GUNTRAIL TO CONDOR

Seth Claybourne, a defeated Confederate soldier with no reason to return home, decided to ride west. Crossing a desert he encountered a man who had been left for dead. Jeb Dawson was still alive, but when his attackers returned, Seth drove them off. Dawson, unfit to travel, wanted Seth to travel to Condor Peaks to validate his claim on valuable land. Vested interests wanted him dead. And being Dawson's proxy put Seth into the firing line . . .

JOHN GLASBY

GUNTRAIL TO CONDOR

Complete and Unabridged

LINFORD
Leicester

First published in Great Britain in 2009 by
Robert Hale Limited
London

First Linford Edition
published 2010
by arrangement with
Robert Hale Limited
London

The moral right of the author has been asserted

British Library CIP Data

Glasby, John S. (John Stephen)
   Guntrail to Condor.- -
   (Linford western library)
   1. Confederate States of America. Army- -
   Fiction. 2. Western stories. 3. Large type books.
   I. Title II. Series
   823.9′14–dc22

2|16 ISBN 978–1–44480–205–4

Published by
F. A. Thorpe (Publishing)
Anstey, Leicestershire

Set by Words & Graphics Ltd.
Anstey, Leicestershire
Printed and bound in Great Britain by
T. J. International Ltd., Padstow, Cornwall

1

The Bushwhackers

The lone rider drifted out of the stand of trees and reined his mount where the trail angled steeply downward, a winding grey scar in the hillside. It ended at the nearer edge of the alkali flats that stretched westward towards a limitless horizon.

A tall, grim-faced man, Seth Claybourne had ridden without rest through the night and now both he and his mount were drooping with fatigue. Barely two months earlier the War between the States had ended in a bitter defeat for the South. Lee had surrendered and now the army was in disarray, scattered across the whole of the southern states.

Some were still fighting. Small bands like those led by Quantrill. But he had

had enough of war, had seen too many good men die, latterly for a lost cause. He still wore the grey uniform of the Confederate Army, now dusty and torn, but he also wore a gunbelt with twin Colts in the holsters. At his back were bands of Northern mercenaries still hunting and killing any Rebs they could find and only a little way behind them were the carpet-baggers from the East, seizing all the land and property they could lay their greedy hands on.

In his pocket he still carried the last letter he had received from his mother telling how the family had been forced off their land and made to leave with what few belongings they could carry. There was no point in him returning home; no reason to go back to nothing. Now he was riding west, struggling to come to terms with the way a few short years had changed his life.

Reining up, he dropped wearily from the saddle. There was a small stream running down the hillside just within the trees and he allowed his horse to drink before swilling the dust from his face and neck. He didn't relish the idea of crossing the wide expanse of alkali but it lay between him and the way he wanted to go. As far as he could determine there was no easy way around it.

Tall, snow-capped mountains barred the way to the north and knowing nothing of this country he couldn't be certain of finding a pass through them.

Seating himself on the grassy bank, in the shade of the tall trees, he ate the last of his food. He knew there would be little enough out in the blazing white wilderness of alkali and little or no water, and possibly he would die of thirst before the hunger got to him.

Stretching himself out on the soft grass, he tipped the brim of his hat over his eyes, feeling the warmth of the sun on his body. Although the sun was just past its zenith and would soon be sinking towards the west, there was no promise of any coolness to come. Some of the bitterness of the Confederate

Army's defeat still rankled in his mind but it was slowly diminishing.

He knew nothing of the territory he was heading into but it must surely be better than returning East. It was new country out there, relatively unexplored in many places. It might be possible for him to find somewhere to put down his roots. He was still reflecting on this possibility when he fell asleep. He woke with his mount nuzzling him in the side. Judging by the way the sun now glinted through the canopy of overhead branches, he estimated he had been asleep for more than three hours. It was time to be moving on. Earlier, he had decided to wait until close to sundown before riding out into that unwelcoming wilderness that stretched before him.

Drinking his fill from the stream and filling his canteen to the brim, he tightened the cinch beneath his mount's belly and swung himself wearily into the saddle. An hour later, the sun was lowering in the cloudless heavens, clipping towards the west. The blistering heat was still in the air that lay, unmoving, all around him, a heavy and settled weight across his back and shoulders.

In every direction there was nothing but the endless flats. He had hoped to come upon some wagon trail that he might follow to the nearest town but all the signs were that no one had been here before him.

Half an hour earlier, he had come upon the dried-out bed of a river. The bed was scarred and ugly with hard-baked clay and dry, brittle vegetation. Now the only vegetation he could see was mesquite and a few patches of sage that somehow managed to suck moisture from deep below the surface.

He experienced a sudden rush of impatience at the slowness of the sun's descent towards the western horizon. If the sky remained clear the temperature would fall, making his progress a little more comfortable. His mouth and throat were parched but he knew he had to conserve his water. Without that a man died very quickly in places like this.

Then, through red-rimmed eyes, he made out the marks, a short distance to his left. Checking his mount, he bent low in the saddle to study them closely. They were clearly delineated in the smooth alkali and the fact that the constantly shifting dust had not covered them told him they had obviously been made recently. One horse and a wagon, he decided finally. The sight of them made him wary, cautious. Reaching down, he eased the heavy Colts in the leather holsters.

Someone had come this way, obviously making for the range of low mountains he could just make out in the distance. Lifting himself in the saddle, he shaded his eyes against the vicious glare of the setting sun, scanning the territory in every direction. He could discern nothing yet he felt certain these tracks had been made not more than a few hours earlier.

Whoever had driven this way it was unlikely they could be too far ahead of him. No one could move fast in the desert with a wagon in tow.

Digging spurs into the weary stallion's flanks, he urged it forward. The sunlight now turned the desert a pale pink that shimmered like smoke, making details difficult to define. Then, less than half a mile ahead, he made out something dark.

Several moments passed before he recognized it as a horse and a small buckboard. The fact that it was clearly not moving sent a little shiver of apprehension through him.

He approached cautiously, his fingers around the butt of the Colt. Only a fool would stop here in the middle of the wilderness unless something drastic had happened. The horse shied away nervously as he drew closer. The man was lying sideways on the seat, his head drooping forward. There was a rifle clutched tightly in his right hand. When the other didn't move at his approach, he guessed the man was dead and relaxed slightly.

Then, without warning, the man pulled himself upright, lifting the rifle until it was trained on Seth's chest.

'Reach for those guns, mister, and I'll plug you.' His voice was little more than a throaty whisper, low in his throat.

Slowly, Seth moved his arms away from his sides. The man looked to be in his sixties with iron-grey hair but in spite of his age, the hand that held the rifle was steady. 'I don't aim to make any trouble,' Seth said slowly, forcing evenness into his tone.

'Guess you came back to make sure I'm dead. Is that it?'

For the first time, Seth made out the red stain on the man's shirt. He shook his head. 'I don't know who did this, friend, but it wasn't me. You look as though you've been hurt real bad and — '

The man leaned forward a little. It was clear to Seth that the effort cost him a lot. Propping himself on one elbow, he kept the weapon on Seth as he raised his other hand weakly to block out some of the sunlight streaming into his eyes.

'You're wearin' a Reb uniform. Then I guess you ain't one o' them killers.'

'I did plenty o' killin' during the war,' Seth said bitterly. 'I don't aim to do any more if I can help it.'

Something like a grin crossed the man's grizzled features. 'Then you're ridin' the wrong trail, son. This is wild territory. It ain't been tamed any more than those who roam these parts.'

'You'd better let me take a look at that shoulder,' Seth said. 'Believe me, I ain't aimin' to kill or rob you.'

Slowly, the man lowered the gun. Swinging down from the saddle, Seth climbed up beside the old man and ripped open his shirt. The slug had taken him in the right shoulder and he'd clearly lost a lot of blood. Tearing off a strip of the man's shirt, he managed to pad the wound, tying it up as best he could.

Going back to his mount, he took down his canteen and gave it to the other. 'Not too much,' he warned. 'We ain't likely to find any more water here.' He waited until the oldster had taken a few sips, then asked, 'Mind tellin' me your name and what you're doin' out here?'

'Jeb Dawson. Like you I fought for the South. When it finished, I aimed to head west.'

'So what happened here? Were you bushwhacked?'

Dawson nodded. 'Three critters jumped me a couple of hours ago. Never had a chance. One of 'em shot me and then they left me for dead. I figured you must be one of 'em. Ain't many folks try to cross this wasteland.'

Seth sank back on to his haunches beside the buckboard. He didn't disbelieve what the other had told him but he had the feeling there was more to it than the man was telling.

'You got any idea why they should've

jumped you?' he asked bluntly, watching the other's eyes closely. 'You don't look to me as though you're carryin' much money.'

Dawson said nothing for a full minute. Then he said, 'You ask a lot o' questions, mister.'

Seth shrugged. 'Guess it's my suspicious nature, friend. The war taught me that. If there's somethin' you don't want to tell me, that's fair enough. But if there are three killers running loose on these flats, killin' just for the hell of it, I'd like to know.'

After a further pause, Dawson said harshly, 'I guess I'll die out here unless you help me. So I figure I have to trust you.'

'Go on.'

'You ever heard o' Condor Peaks?'

Seth shook his head. 'Nope. Is that where you were headed?'

Dawson licked his lips. 'It's a stretch o' land some hundred miles north-west o' here. Before the war came, I bought that land from the government. I still have the deeds but it seems some other folk want it now.'

Seth sat back and waited for the other to continue. Even the effort of talking seemed to have cost him a lot. Finally, however, he sucked in a deep, racking breath and went on, 'Those men who jumped me, they're workin' hand in hand with the railroad. Seems my land at Condor Peaks is plumb in the middle o' where they want to run the new line. Without it, they'd have to detour more'n fifty miles to the north.'

'And you're not willin' to sell, is that it?'

'I might think o' sellin' if I was offered the right price but what they were willin' to pay was only a tenth o' what it's worth.'

Seth gave a nod of understanding. 'So they decided to hire some killers to get those deeds for free?'

'You guessed right, mister.'

'And did they get the deeds when they jumped you?'

Dawson forced a weak grin. 'I meant

to make camp here for the night and before I settled down, I buried 'em in the alkali. They never found 'em but when you came I figured they'd come back to make sure I was dead and to take a second look.'

'So you still have them?'

Lifting a hand, Dawson pointed to a spot where a clump of brittle sage grew out of the ground.

At the other's nod, Seth walked over and began scooping away the alkali. He found the small leather pouch a couple of minutes later and took it back to the old man. Fumbling inside it, Dawson drew out a crumpled document and handed it to him.

Seth perused it carefully in the brilliant sunlight. It was evidently a map. Condor Peaks was marked on it and several other features. He saw enough to recognize it was also a legitimate bill of sale for the land around Condor Peaks.

Giving it back to the other, Seth said, 'If what you say is true, I guess I can understand why the railroad wants your land. But I think things have changed a little after the war. From what little I know, you have to claim it in person within a certain time or it reverts back to the government. Have you thought about that?'

'Sure. I was aimin' to set out in a couple o' days but it doesn't look as if I'm goin' to make it now.'

Looking up at Dawson, Seth said sharply, 'You reckon you'll be all right if I take the reins? I'll tie my mount to the back.'

Dawson swallowed thickly and then gave a weak nod. 'I'll try, friend, but it ain't goin' to do either of us any good.' He jerked a feeble hand in the direction of the flats. 'We'll never make it that way. Too many men have died tryin' to cross that wilderness.'

'Then have you got any better suggestion?' Seth asked.

'The only way is north-west. Skirt around the flats. There's a narrow pass through yon mountains. I was tryin' to make for it when those critters jumped me.'

After tying the bay to the back of the buckboard, Seth climbed on to the seat beside Dawson. By now, the old man was drooping to one side, his eyes closed to mere slits. He was barely conscious but somehow, by clutching tightly to his left, he remained upright against the jolting motion. Shading his eyes with one hand, Seth scanned the nearby terrain for any sign of a waterhole — but there was nothing.

This was clearly a land that wanted nothing of Man; a barren wilderness that had been there for millennia and would never change.

Taking his canteen where it lay beside him, he held it out to Dawson, keeping a tight grip on the reins and steadying the other with his shoulder. The man tried desperately to swallow but evidently his throat was so parched as to make this almost impossible. Much of the precious water spilled from his mouth and dribbled down his chin but he got enough down him to give a slight nod of thanks and hand the canteen back.

By the time the sun went down in a fiery red glow, bringing a little coolness from the east, they had almost reached the hills. Long, jagged, black shadows spread across the white alkali. Seth dismounted and helped Dawson from the buckboard, stretching him out on the ground.

Squinting up at him, Dawson said in a low whisper, 'Why are you stoppin' here? The pass is only about two miles away in that direction.' He lifted an arm to point. 'We might as well travel through the night while it's cool.'

'There are three men somewhere out there,' Seth reminded him. 'Since they didn't find what they were lookin' for it's possible they might come back for a second look. I'd sooner keep watch for them out here in the open than among those hills.'

'You're just wastin' precious time and water with me, son,' Dawson grunted.

He tried to push himself up on to his arms but then fell back with a low groan. 'I ain't goin' to make it to a doctor. It's a ways to Cranton even if we get through the pass and there's no guarantee o' that.'

Seth looked at his companion sharply. In the darkening dusk, the man's face was just a pale blur. 'What do you mean by that, old-timer?' he asked harshly.

'I mean those critters didn't just come up on me out here. Somebody knew where I was and that somebody sent 'em. Like you just said, if there's any place along the road to Cranton where more of 'em will lie in wait, it'll be somewhere along that pass.'

'But is there any reason why anyone should try another ambush? As far as they know, you're dead and they know nothin' o' me.'

'They want those deeds and they'll go to any lengths to get their hands on them. They know I had 'em when I left Twin Creeks three days ago and they must've stuck to my trail like leeches.'

'Then I reckon we'll bed down here for the night. It's plenty open and if any o' them do decide to come along, we'll see 'em far off.'

There was no chance of building a fire. A blaze would be spotted for miles, particularly if there were sharp eyes watching this trail. Getting some jerky from his saddle-bag, he handed a piece to Dawson, They chewed on it for a while in silence, each man engrossed in his own thoughts. A few moments later, Dawson lay back and closed his eyes.

With the darkness came the silence, the deep unsettling silence of the wilderness. The sky sentinels were out in their thousands but thankfully there was no moon.

The night grew colder and going to his mount, Seth took down his bedroll and spread it on the alkali. But he didn't stretch himself out on it. Instead, he sat on his haunches, staring up at the stars. Was there any truth in what this old man claimed? Certainly the deeds seemed authentic and now that the war was over, the railroad would be building lines across the entire country.

A sudden sound intruded upon the stillness. Gently, Seth eased himself to his knees and stared into the darkness. He could see nothing but a quiet snicker from his mount warned him that the stallion had also scented danger. Lowering himself on to his chest, he eased the Colts from their holsters and pulled back the hammers.

He spotted the movement a couple of minutes later — two riders heading towards him from the direction of the pass. From the way they were bending low in the saddle, it was clear they were searching for something, possibly looking for any sign of a trail.

Very slowly, Seth eased himself up on to one elbow and in that same moment, one of the men gave a sudden yell and pointed directly at the buckboard. Clearly, these men had figured there was only a badly wounded man to contend with for they stepped down from their saddles without any haste.

Seth could hear them talking among themselves as they came forward, obviously expecting no trouble.

'Hold it right there,' Seth called harshly. 'Both of you.'

He saw the man halt abruptly. Then both of them went for their guns. The Colts in Seth's hands spoke twice. The shorter of the men jerked as the slug took him in the chest. He stood for a moment, arms hanging limply at his sides. Then his weapons dropped from his nerveless fingers and he pitched forward on to the alkali.

The second man had been quicker, diving to one side and rolling over to his left. Seth saw the muzzle flash and heard the wicked hum of a slug close to his cheek a split second later. The man had somehow found a shallow hollow and dropped into it. Two more shots passed dangerously close above Seth's head as he hugged the ground.

Now the positions were reversed. So long as the other kept his head down, it would be virtually impossible to hit him whereas Seth was lying out in the open, completely exposed. Seth lay absolutely still, holding the Colts steady, sighting them on the spot where the man had disappeared. The silence grew more intense. Now it was going to be a case of who broke first.

Inwardly, he hoped that Dawson wouldn't make any stupid move if he'd been woken by the sound of the shots. But there came no movement from the oldster and Seth guessed he had lost consciousness.

From where he lay, Seth could just pick out the other killer's harsh breathing. The gunhawk was getting nervous. Then the man made his play. Jerking himself on to one elbow, he fired three times in quick succession before thrusting himself to his feet and making a run for his mount.

Seth felt one of the slugs pluck at his hat brim. Then he swung the Colts, took quick aim and squeezed the triggers. He saw the dark shape suddenly halt in mid-stride, saw the other's arms reach upward, high above his head, as if he were clawing for the sky. Then he pitched forward on to his face and lay still.

Glancing round, Seth saw that Dawson was awake, peering into the darkness. Bending Seth caught the dead man by the neck of his jacket and dragged him over to where Dawson lay.

'Is this one of those *hombres* who bushwhacked you?' he asked harshly.

With an effort, Dawn leaned forward and stared at the man's swarthy features, then gave a quick, jerky nod of affirmation. 'That's one of 'em,' he said. 'What happened to the others? There were three of 'em.'

'His friend is also dead over yonder.' Seth jerked his thumb towards the other dead killer. 'There were only two of 'em. No sign of a third man.'

'Then I guess he's somewhere out there, still watchin' the trail. Either that, or he's ridden on into Cranton, leaving these two to deal with me.'

Thrusting fresh shells into the Colts,

Seth muttered, 'They must be pretty certain you've still got these deeds they're after.'

'That's evidently what they're bein' paid for.'

'I see.' Seth sank down on to the alkali and stared musingly at the dead man a few feet away. If these men were so determined to get their hands on that piece of paper, it was just possible that there was something in what this old man said after all. 'Reckon you'd better get some sleep old-timer,' he said finally.

'What do we do with these two?' asked the other.

'I'll bury 'em in the mornin'. It's either that or leave 'em to the buzzards.'

Dawson said nothing more but rolled over on to his back and closed his eyes.

★   ★   ★

With the dawn there came a sudden change in the weather. Dark, menacing thunderheads brooded over the tops of

23

the mountains and the air took on a chilly feel. A wind had got up, lifting the alkali, blowing it in stinging gusts into their faces as they moved slowly towards the pass. Dawson still drooped beside him on the buckboard, at times barely conscious, but the night's sleep seemed to have done him some little good.

The storm broke just as they entered the pass, with a vicious gale funnelling between the steeply rising walls of rock. Rain struck them from every direction and within minutes both men were drenched to the skin. Leaning sideways, Seth pressed his mouth close to Dawson's ear and yelled, 'We've got to find someplace out o' this storm and wait until it passes over.'

He saw the other give an almost imperceptible nod and knew that he understood. Slitting his eyes against the wind, Seth scanned the rocks on either side of the trail. For the most part they rose, smooth and unbroken, from the canyon floor but then he spotted a dark shadow a few yards ahead.

Swiftly, he turned the horse towards it. Two minutes later they had pulled off the trail and were in the comparative safety of the deep, wide cleft in the rock, sheltered from most of the wind. Letting go of the reins, Seth checked on his companion. The front of his shirt was stained with fresh blood and his features had assumed a greyish look. It was clear the man was bleeding internally and unless he got him to a doctor pretty soon, there was no chance for him.

'Don't try to get down,' he urged, as Dawson attempted to lift himself from the seat. 'If you do, I doubt whether you'll be in any condition to get back on. We'll just rest here until this storm passes over.'

He saw Dawson give a weak nod, his fingers still clamped tightly around the wooden pole by his side. Moving to the mouth of the opening, Seth peered into the teeming rain. It was then he picked out the sound in the distance, the unmistakable pounding of hoof-beats coming rapidly closer.

Swiftly, he jerked a Colt from its holster and pressed himself close against the rock. The only thought in his mind was that this was the third bushwhacker; that somehow the killer had found the rough graves of his companions and was now trailing them.

A few moments later, the rider came into sight, head bent low against the wind. Seth waited tensely, then stepped out into the open, the Colt levelled, his finger hard on the trigger.

'Hold it right there, mister,' he called loudly. 'Don't try to go for your guns.'

With an effort, the rider controlled the suddenly bucking mount. One hand went up but only to throw back the hood. Seth uttered a low gasp of stunned surprise. Long chestnut hair cascaded down the girl's back as she stared down at him.

Her clear gaze look in the Confederate uniform as she sat quite still in the saddle. Then she said, 'You can put your gun away. I'm not one of your Northerners.'

Slowly, Seth lowered the Colt and then thrust it back into its holster. 'Then what are you doin' here?'

'I'm looking for my father. He went out nearly a week ago and never returned. He was going to see some lawyer to check on some old deeds he had. I'm afraid something may have happened to him.'

Seth opened his mouth to ask a further question but at that moment, a faint shout came from behind him. 'Is that you, Belle?'

The girl jerked up her head, then slid swiftly from the saddle, pushing past Seth. Going up to the old man she grasped him tightly by the arm, then swung on Seth. 'What happened to him? Who shot him?'

'I came upon him yesterday, out in the wastelands. He'd been shot and left for dead. I'm trying to get him to a doctor but I don't know if he'll last out that long. He's lost quite a lot o' blood.'

'There's Doc Felder in Cranton. We'll have to get him there. Will you help me?'

Seth gave a wry grin. 'I've brought him this far. I guess I'll stick with him though I had to kill a couple of men who came back to make sure he was dead.'

Wrinkling her brow, the girl said harshly, 'But why would anyone want to kill him?'

Seth shrugged. 'Maybe he has something they wanted.'

He noticed the sudden gust of expression that flashed across her features. 'You mean those deeds he carries about with him? I don't know why he persists in believing they're genuine. I know Martin Shelton, he's the lawyer in Cranton, maintains they are but unless he gets to this place, Condor Peaks, within the next three weeks, he loses all right to that land.'

'You may be right. But those three who ambushed him out there in the badlands weren't going to take any chances o' that happening.' Seth paused as another thought struck him. 'Did you see anyone out on the trail yonder?'

Belle shook her head. 'No. You reckon there may be others after him?'

'I'm sure of it. He said three men bushwhacked him. Like I told you, I killed two when they came back durin' the night. I guess the third man must've ridden on into Cranton. If that's the case, we'd better tread warily once we get there.'

The girl didn't answer him but turned all of her attention on her father. 'That slug is in pretty deep. We can't afford to waste time talking.' Without another word she moved towards her mount and made to swing lithely into the saddle.

'Might I suggest, miss, that you take the buckboard. You know this trail better than I do.'

Giving a quick nod of agreement, Belle climbed on to the seat beside her father, while Seth untied the stallion and climbed quickly into the saddle, leading Belle's horse by the reins.

Moving in single file with Seth bringing up the rear where he could keep an eye on the other two, they headed out into the full fury of the storm. Lightning cracked across the heavens, thunder roared in their ears and the rain still came down in torrents. Underfoot, the trail became a river making it difficult for the horses to keep their footing.

Then, almost as swiftly as it had come, the storm ceased. The sun came out, hot and brilliant. Squinting through the glare, Seth noticed where the trail now turned abruptly south across a low ridge and widened considerably.

He urged his mount forward as Belle called, 'My advice would be to get rid of that Reb uniform as soon as you can. Cranton is now full of Northerners and they don't take too kindly to strangers dressed like that.'

'Is there no law at all in this town?' Seth asked.

She shook her head. 'None to speak

of. Sam Willis is the sheriff and I guess he does his best. But Herb Bentley is the real law in town.'

From the way she spoke the name Seth reckoned she had no liking for Bentley. 'What sort o' man is he?'

'Bentley? He virtually runs the town. Owns most of it. He has three saloons and most of the spreads to the north and east. He's well in with the railroad men. My guess is he's trying to get the railroad to come through Cranton. If that happens, the land he owns will be worth a fortune.'

Seth thought that over, then said, 'You think that Bentley might know of this deed your father has.'

Belle pursed her lips. 'It's possible, I suppose. But what difference would that make? Condor Peaks is well over a hundred miles from here.'

'I was just thinking that if those railroad men are so interested in gettin' your father's land, Bentley might be in cahoots with 'em.'

By now they had reached the top of

the ridge and looking down, Seth saw Cranton spread out across the valley below them. It looked little different from a score of other towns he had seen along the frontier, wild and sprawling.

Checking her mount, Belle said harshly, 'I've been thinking. It might not be wise for us to head straight into town. We have a small spread yonder. I reckon we should head there first and I'll have one of the boys ride into town for Doc Felder. We have a couple of men working for us and I think you could get a better outfit than that Confederate uniform from one of them.'

She pulled sharply on the reins and swung the buckboard abruptly to the right, keeping to the side of the ridge, out of sight of anyone down below. Fifteen minutes later, she led the way through a wide gate and on to the courtyard of a small homestead. There was smoke issuing from the chimney and a moment later a tall, broad-shouldered man came out on to the wooden veranda. At Belle's call, he ran quickly forward.

'My father's been shot,' the girl said tautly. 'Help us get him into the house.'

Gently, they eased Dawson from the seat and carried him into the front room of the house, settling him into a chair. He was still conscious but his grizzled features had assumed a greyish cast.

Turning to the tall man, Belle said, 'I want you to ride into town, Clint, and bring Doctor Felder. Tell him it's urgent and what's happened.'

Clint gave a quick nod. 'I'll do that right away, Miss Belle.' He went out and a moment later, Seth saw him through the window spurring his mount swiftly across the courtyard. Then he turned his attention to the man lying slumped in the chair.

'Don't you think we should try to get him on to the bed?' Belle asked anxiously.

Shaking his head, Seth said firmly, 'No. I reckon it would be best to leave him here, at least until the doctor gets here. How long do you think it'll take before he arrives.'

'Half an hour. If they have any sense they'll take the long trail from town over the hills.'

'Meaning that you figure someone might be watching the doctor's place and follow them.'

'After what's happened, I think that's highly likely.' She tried to keep the worry out of her voice but Seth could see she was close to tears.

'Your father will make it,' he said, forcing conviction into his voice.

'I'll make you something to eat,' she said abruptly, changing the subject. 'When was the last time you had a decent meal?'

'So long ago I can't rightly remember,' Seth replied.

She went into the kitchen and a few minutes later brought through a plate heaped with bacon, sausages and a couple of eggs. Seating herself in the chair opposite, she waited until he had finished, then asked, 'What brings you here to Cranton? I can tell you're not one of those railroad men, or a carpet-bagger.'

Building himself a smoke, he leaned back and lit it. 'When the war ended, I figured on going back to Virginia but my parents wrote to tell me that we no longer had the ranch. The Northerners took everything we had. There was nothing there for me to go back for so I decided to head west. That's how I came across your father out there in the Badlands.'

'I'm real glad you did otherwise he'd have been dead by now. Here, at least, he has a fighting chance if only the doctor would get here.'

Belle cleared away the dishes and then stood by the window, her hands clasped behind her back, staring out into the distance. Seth watched her from beneath lowered lids. Here, he thought, was a woman who faced up to all obstacles in her path, was willing to fight for what was hers.

It was a little while later, when he heard her give a sharp exclamation. 'They're back,' she said harshly, 'but it seems we have a visitor as well.'

Seth got to his feet and joined her at the window in time to see the three men who rode into the courtyard. He guessed the small man with grey hair to be the doctor. Beside him was a tall, hard-faced man. As the latter stepped down from the saddle the sunlight glinted on the star on his shirt.

'Seems they have the sheriff in tow,' Seth remarked. 'I wonder what he wants.'

'Perhaps to question you and my father as to what happened,' Belle suggested. 'Take care what you say to him. He's a good man and tries to keep the law in town but he's just one man and I'm not certain how far I can trust him. Besides, we don't get many dressed like you in Cranton.'

Before she could say anything further the door opened and the doctor came in, closely followed by the lawman. The latter threw a swift glance in Seth's direction but beyond a brief expression of surprise, said nothing.

Going over to the chair, Felder knelt beside Dawson and pulled open his shirt. His lips tightened as he examined the wound. Then he looked round at Belle. 'Boil me some water and get me a towel,' he said crisply.

As she moved towards the kitchen, he added, 'And a bottle of whiskey. He's goin' to need it.'

'Do you reckon you can get that slug out, Doc?' Seth asked.

Felder stared hard at Seth and there was a hint of suspicion on his angular features. 'Just who are you, mister? I see you're wearin' a Reb uniform.'

'That's what I was about to ask,' Willis interrupted. 'You know who shot Dawson?'

Seth felt a sudden rush of anger at the sheriff's tone but fought it down. 'No, Sheriff, I don't. When I came upon him in the wilderness, he told me three men had ambushed him. When two of 'em came back to make sure he was dead, I killed 'em and buried 'em out there. I figure the third *hombre* must be somewhere in town. By now, he'll be wonderin' what happened to his friends.'

'And what's your name and business in Cranton?'

'The name's Claybourne, Seth Claybourne. I was a lieutenant in the Confederate Army. When the war ended I decided to head west. As far as Cranton is concerned, I merely intended gettin' some supplies and ridin' on.'

The sheriff gave a terse nod. 'Somehow, I reckon that would be the be thing to do. There are a lot o' folk in town who don't like Southerners. Especially any who — ' He broke off sharply as Belle came back with a basin of water.

In the chair, Dawson was now barely conscious, his head lolling to one side. Felder placed the whiskey bottle to his lips. 'Better get some o' this down you,

Jeb, it'll help to dull the pain. That slug is in deep and mighty close to your lung.'

'Just get it out, Doc, and bandage me up,' Dawson muttered in a throaty whisper, 'I've got a lot o' things to do and all of 'em in a mighty big hurry.'

'You won't be doin' anything in a hurry. Even if you live, you'll still need plenty o' rest.' The doctor turned to Belle. 'And it's up to you to see that he gets it.'

'I'll do my best, Doctor, but you know what he's like when he gets his mind set on something.'

'I know he's a stubborn old cuss but this time he has to do as he's told. Now just lie quiet. This ain't goin' to be easy.'

Dawson uttered a low moan as the doctor began probing and a couple of minutes later his head lolled to one side, his eyes closed.

'He's unconscious,' Felder said in reply to Belle's look of mute inquiry. 'Guess it's better that way.'

Deftly, the doctor went to work, his lips pressed into a tight line of concentration. Several minutes passed and then he gave a grunt of satisfaction. Slowly, he withdrew the small forceps and dropped something on to the table.

'That's it done,' he said harshly. 'Now I'll just have to bandage him up and the rest is up to him.'

'Do you think he's going to pull through?' Belle asked anxiously.

'If he gets through the next couple o' days, I figure he'll make it. He's damned lucky to be alive with that slug in him.' The doctor glanced up at Seth. 'It was fortunate you found him when you did, mister, and got him here. I doubt if he'd have survived another day in that wilderness.'

Seth nodded. 'Whoever those men were who were after him, they certainly didn't want him to live,' he said grimly. 'And there's still that third man somewhere in town. He certainly won't rest until he gets what he was after.' He noticed the warning look on the girl's face and said nothing more.

Once the doctor had finished, he snapped his bag shut and said, 'If he's hungry when he wakes up, give him some soup. If you can get him into bed, it'll help. Now he needs all the rest he can get.'

'I'll do what I can, Doc.' Seth said.

'I thought you said you were just ridin' through.' There was a grim note to the sheriff's voice. 'This town ain't healthy for strangers.'

'Reckon I'll stay until I'm sure the old man gets on his feet again,' Seth replied.

The lawman was silent for several moments and it was clear to Seth that his reply was not what the other wanted to hear. Finally, Willis nodded. 'All right, mister. But the sooner you get rid o' that uniform, the better.'

'I'll get you something to change into,' Belle said. 'After all you've done for my father it's the least I can do. You can bunk down with the boys.'

As the sheriff made to leave with the

doctor, Seth said sharply, 'You got any idea who this third man might be, Sheriff?'

Willis stopped in his tracks and there was an expression on his face that Seth couldn't analyse. 'I reckon it could be one of several men. Right now there are possibly a dozen men working on behalf of the railroad in Cranton. Only Jeb here could recognize him and he ain't likely to talk for a while.'

2

Dangerous Trails

It was two days later when Seth had a talk with Dawson. The other was now fully conscious, fretting with impatience at his enforced stay in bed. Seth had waited until Belle had left the bedroom and then questioned the older man regarding his claim to Condor Peaks.

'I'd say there's no doubt this document you have is genuine,' he told Dawson. 'Your daughter told me that the lawyer fellow in town says the same. But as you have to present yourself in person, right now it's virtually worthless.'

'You reckon I don't know that?' Jeb's voice was as close to a shout as he could manage. 'And to have to lie here means one day less in which to do it. Goddamnit, Seth! It's more'n a hundred miles from here and across some o' the worst country there is.'

'And you can be sure those railroad men will do all they can to stop you.'

'Then you reckon I should give up?' Dawson shook his head vehemently, grimaced as a lance of pain shot through his shoulder.

'That depends on how much you trust me, old-timer.'

'Trust you? You saved my life out there. Just what are you sayin'?'

Seth remained silent for several moments, then said, 'You've got to realize that it'll be quite a while before you're on your feet again and be able to ride. But that clerk at Condor ain't seen you before. If I was to take that document and register it in your name then — '

'Why should we trust you to do that?' Belle had returned and was standing in the doorway.

Seth shrugged. 'I figure it's the only chance you've got. Once your pa is fully recovered, he can ride north to Condor.'

'To find that you've already got your name on that land register.' Belle's face was set in angry, suspicious lines. 'We know almost nothing about you. For all we know you could be just another drifter looking to make an easy fortune.'

Seth bit down on the angry retort that rose to his lips. 'If you feel that way, miss, then forget what I said. But the harsh fact is that someone must reach Condor before this time limit expires and you sure can't pass yourself off as your father.'

'Easy now, Belle,' her father said hoarsely. 'Don't go shootin' your mouth off afore we've considered this. There's a whole heap o' sense in what he says.'

'There's only one way I'd ever agree to this,' Belle snapped, 'and that is if I go with him.'

'Well?' Dawson looked up at Seth.

'Hell, Jeb! That's bad country out there and don't forget there are still men out there who desperately want to get their hands on those papers.'

'If you're thinking this way because

I'm a woman,' the girl said harshly, 'then forget it. I can ride as well as any man and shoot just as fast.'

'What do you reckon, Jeb?' Seth asked.

'She's just like her mother,' the older man replied. 'Once she sets her mind on somethin', nothing will stop her goin' through with it.'

Seth spread his hands in a gesture of resignation. 'Then I reckon it should take us about a week to reach Condor Peaks from here, mebbe less if we ride hard and fast. That gives us a little time in which to make some preparations.'

'Why wait that long?' Jeb jerked himself upright in the bed. 'There ain't any time to waste. Surely it makes sense to leave tomorrow.'

'Just hold your horses for a minute and think, Jeb,' Seth retorted. 'We'll need grub and water as well as ammunition.'

'That will only take a couple of hours,' Belle put in. 'Why wait any longer?'

Seth stared down at the old man. 'In case you've both forgotten, there's a man in Cranton who wants those papers and he'll kill you to get them. My guess is that he'll know by now that you're still alive and he'll come very soon — and almost certainly he won't be alone.'

'I suspect that none of your hired hands is a gunman and after what happened to the man's two colleagues in the Badlands, he'll have more friends with him. In a town like this he can easily hire a handful o' gunslingers to ride with him. You wouldn't stand a chance against 'em.'

'So what do you suggest we do?' Belle asked, seating herself carefully on the edge of the bed.

'Well, first we'll need grub and water as well as ammunition. I'll ride into town for what we need.' To Belle, he said firmly, 'You stay here with your pa. Nobody knows me in town but I guess about everyone knows you. It'll be less dangerous this way and fewer questions might be asked.'

'That makes sense, Belle,' Jeb muttered. 'If you go folk might figure these vittles are for me and we're getting' ready to make a journey o' some kind. Seth here ain't known in town. All he has to say is that he's just passing through and needs 'em for wherever he's headed.'

'Then it's settled,' Seth muttered. 'I'll make out a list of all we'll need and saddle up. It shouldn't take much more'n an hour to get there and back.' He could see that the girl was still unsure of him but she said nothing. 'Just one thing,' he added finally, 'Do you reckon either the sheriff or that doctor will have talked about me bein' here?'

'That ain't likely,' Jeb acknowledged.

★ ★ ★

Reining the stallion on a low rise overlooking the town, Seth leaned forward in the saddle and built himself a smoke. Life in the Confederate Army had taught him caution. From his vantage point he could see there was a lot of activity on the streets. Several mounts were tethered to the hitching rails outside the saloons.

His keen gaze caught something else. There were more frock-coated men around than was usual in these frontier towns. Evidently a lot of important business went on in Cranton and he wondered just how many of these men were working for the railroad. It was unlikely that third man who had attacked Dawson would connect him with what had happened to those other two men but he didn't mean to take any chances.

Finishing his smoke, he tossed the butt away and set his mount to the smooth downgrade. He had already decided that he would first pay a call on the sheriff. If anyone might help him identify that killer, the lawman would know more of what went on in town than almost anyone else.

He found the sheriff's office halfway along the street, almost directly opposite the largest of the saloons. Dropping from the saddle, he looped the reins over the rail and stepped up on to the boardwalk, aware that several of the folk nearby were watching him curiously. Pushing open the door, he went inside.

Willis was seated behind his desk, his feet resting on it. An expression of surprise flashed over his grizzled features as he saw who his visitor was.

'Claybourne! What the hell are you doin' in town? I thought you were ridin' on once old Jeb got over the worst.'

'I've changed my mind. But for your information I'm only in town to collect some food and ammunition. I'll be gone within the next few days.'

Willis looked relieved at that statement and leaned back. 'Now you're showin' some sense. Like I told you before, Cranton ain't a healthy place for strangers.'

'Now why should that be, Sheriff?'

Seth inquired smoothly. Without being asked, he sat down in the other chair, took off his hat and placed it on the desk in front of him. 'It seems to me just like an ordinary frontier town. No better and no worse than others I've known.'

Willis took a bottle and two glasses from the top drawer of his desk. Pouring some of the liquor into both glasses, he pushed one towards Seth. 'There's been a lot o' trouble in town recently,' he said harshly. 'Ever since word got around that the railroad were considerin' building a branch line here to link us with the main line forty miles away. There are a lot o' folk here who are against it and a few who want it.'

'And those who want it are the men who own the land it would cross since they'd make a fortune selling that land to the company.'

'That's about the size of it,' Willis agreed. 'And these men are also grabbing land from the smaller cattlemen. There's a range war in the makin'' and I don't want to be in the middle of it but as sheriff I have to keep the peace and uphold the law. You look like a man who knows how to handle a gun. I don't suppose you'd consider the job o' my deputy.'

'Unfortunately, I've got urgent business out o' town, Sheriff. Like I told you, I'm headin' west. The reason I came to see you is to ask if there's any lone rider come into town within the last few days.'

The lawman gave him a shrewd glance. 'You still looking for that *hombre* who bushwhacked Jeb Dawson?'

'I figure he's still here in Cranton.'

Willis scratched his chin. 'Plenty o' strangers ride in here. They stay for a couple o' days and then drift on, except of course for those who sign on for Herb Bentley. You ain't got any idea what he looks like, have you?'

'Afraid not.' Seth shook his head. 'I never saw him but I've got the feelin' he's still after Jeb.'

'I can't figure why they tried to kill

him. All he has is tied up in that small spread of his.'

'Do you know if anyone has tried to buy it from him?'

Willis thought for a while, then nodded. 'I heard that Clem Henders made him an offer. It was a good offer at that. But I reckon you know Jeb by now. He's a stubborn old cuss and refused to sell.'

Seth finished his drink and set his glass down on the desk. Getting to his feet, he said, 'Well, thanks for the drink, Sheriff, and for the information. It's been most useful.'

Willis gave a short nod. 'Just remember what I told you before. Watch your back while you're in town. If you're not in with Henders or Bentley, you'll be regarded with suspicion.'

'I will,' Seth promised.

Stepping on to the boardwalk, he made his way across the street to the nearest saloon. The sound of a tinny old piano reached him as he pushed open the batwing doors. Even at that time of the day the place was crowded. As he made his way to the bar, he kept his glance fixed on the long mirror at the back. There he could see everything without giving himself away.

Several of the men there were dressed in black frock coats. Very few were ordinary cowhands and the latter seemed to be gathered in one group, occupying the two tables nearest the doors.

'What's your pleasure, mister?' The bartender had moved towards him, running a cloth over the top of the counter.

'Whiskey,' Seth said quietly. He was acutely aware of the sudden increase in tension inside the room.

Coming back with a bottle and glass the man placed them in front of him. Seth took out a couple of coins and tossed them on to the counter, watching the other closely as he picked them up.

'You lookin' for a job or just ridin' through, stranger?' The tall man had appeared suddenly at Seth's elbow. He wore a long black frockcoat like many of the others Seth had seen. There was a diamond pin in his necktie clearly intended to give the impression of importance. A short distance behind him stood another man, obviously a Mexican.

Seth shrugged. 'I'm just in town to buy some vittles and then I'll be ridin' out in a couple o' days or so.'

'A pity. I've always prided myself on bein' a good judge o' men. Isn't that right, Reno?' He turned to the man beside him who merely smiled, showing his small, even teeth.

'And I had you figured for a man who knows how to handle a gun. Someone who can take orders without askin' too many questions.'

Seth shook his head. 'Sorry, mister. I take orders from no one and as I said before, I ain't lookin' for a job.'

'Then you'll be staying at the hotel while you're here?' It was more of a question than a statement and Seth had the feeling the man was trying to extract information from him. The thought started a warning bell ringing in his mind.

Speaking casually, he said, 'You ask a lot o' questions, mister. I've just ridden into town. Once I've finished my business, I'll be ridin' out again.'

A smile appeared on the other's face but his eyes belied any attempt at friendliness. They were cold and calculating. 'My name's Bentley. Since I own most o' this town, I like to know as much as I can about any strangers who come ridin' in. We sometimes get men comin' here intent on making trouble and that isn't good for business. I hope you're not one of them.'

Seth swallowed half of his whiskey before saying tautly, 'I never aim to cause trouble, Mister Bentley, but if it finds me, I sure as hell finish it.'

He noticed the flush on Bentley's swarthy features, saw his fingers curl into a fist. Then, with an effort, the other forced control over himself. 'May I ask which way you came when you rode into town? Perhaps you headed across the Badlands and then through the pass.'

Seth knew why that particular question had been asked. Bentley somehow knew that Dawson had been ambushed out there in the desert and was fishing for details, uncertain as to how two gunslingers could have gone missing when they apparently faced only a solitary old-timer.

His first thought, that Bentley was the third man who had bushwhacked Dawson was instantly dismissed: Bentley was not the type to risk his life. He had plenty of money to pay others for that to be done.

'What's so important about the trail I took?'

'Nothing, just interested.' There was a crafty expression on the other's face now as if he were wondering whether he had said more than he intended. 'But if you value your health I suggest you be out o' Cranton by this time tomorrow.'

'And if I'm not?'

'Then you'll find that this town can be a very dangerous and unhealthy place.' Bentley turned on his heel and glanced at the Mexican. 'Reno here has his own ways of dealin' with anyone who might be unwillin' to see reason.'

Deliberately ignoring the two men, Seth turned back to the bar, and picked up his glass. To the barkeep, he said quietly, 'Is it always like this, friend?'

In the mirror he saw the Mexican flush angrily at the insult implied by Seth's action. His hand dropped swiftly towards his belt. Before he could draw out the long-bladed knife that rested there, he found himself looking down the barrel of Seth's gun.

'You're a little too slow, Reno,' Seth said smoothly, a note of menace in his voice. Reaching forward, he pulled out the knife, spun it once in the air, catching it by the tip. His left arm went back and then forward. The knife flashed across the room and embedded itself high in the opposite wall near the ceiling.

'Like I just said, Mister Bentley, I don't go lookin' for trouble but if it comes, I sure as hell finish it. I reckon the two of you had better leave before I decide to use this gun.'

'You ain't heard the last o' this, stranger.' Bentley snarled the words. 'Believe me, you won't walk out o' Cranton alive.'

Seth watched them leave, the doors swinging shut behind them. Then he turned back to the bar.

The bartender ran his tongue around his lips and made a show of wiping the counter with a rag. 'I'd watch your step, mister.' He spoke so softly it was doubtful if anyone else heard him. 'Nobody talks to Herb Bentley like that and gets away with it.'

Seth leaned forward and in a low conspiratorial whisper said, 'Tell me, how does Bentley stand with regard to the railroad and the proposed link with Cranton?'

The barkeep swung his glance around the room and then began to scrub the counter even more vigorously than before. 'Anythin' I tell you, you keep to yourself, mister.'

'Sure,' Seth nodded.

'It's true that Bentley and a couple of his friends have been buying up land around the town for the past six months. Trouble is, he doesn't care how he gets it. A whole heap o' the smaller ranchers have been forced to sell out at a tenth o' the worth of their land. Those who didn't had their cattle rustled and barns burned to the ground.'

'And where does this guy Henders fit in?'

'Nobody knows much about him,' the barkeep remarked drily. 'Some figure that he's workin' for Bentley, buyin' land under his own name and then passin' it on to Bentley. Others reckon he's against the railroad for some reason and is tryin' to stop it from comin' to Cranton.'

Seth finished his drink and went

outside on to the boardwalk. Leaning against one of the wooden uprights, he rolled himself a smoke. What he had just heard merely confirmed what Dawson had told him.

Across the street, he saw that Bentley had stopped and was in deep conversation with two other men. There was no sign of the Mexican but Seth guessed he wouldn't be very far away. One glance at them told Seth that these were not railroad men. Both had the unmistakable look of a gunfighter about them.

One of them lifted his head and stared directly at Seth. Then he looked away quickly and concentrated on what Bentley was saying.

Lighting the cigarette with a sulphur match, Seth kept his gaze on the three men until Bentley moved away and went into the hotel a short distance along the street. Inwardly, Seth knew that any trouble would not come from Bentley. He paid men to do his killing for him.

A moment later, one of the gunmen moved to the far side of the street, stepped on to the boardwalk and stood leaning against the wall, his hands close to the Colts at his sides. The other sauntered slowly in Seth's direction.

Blowing smoke into the air, Seth tossed the cigarette butt into the dirt. This was an old Indian trick, one he had seen often before. Divide your forces so that if one man didn't get you, the other would.

The gunhawk stopped when he was ten feet away, his eyes narrowed against the vicious sunlight. He held his hands low, close to the butts of the Colts at his waist. 'It seems you don't like the kind o' job Mister Bentley offered you, mister,' he said harshly.

Seth stiffened. It was clear these two gunfighters were ready to make trouble and he didn't doubt the order had come from Bentley. Thinly, he said, 'Maybe I don't mind the job, friend, it's just Bentley I don't like.'

'Well in this town, folks do as Mister Bentley says.'

'Does that apply to everyone who rides into this town?' Seth asked smoothly.

'Guess it does.'

From the edge of his vision, Seth saw the sheriff step out of his office but the lawman made no move to intervene. Willis knew what was about to happen but he seemed willing to stand by and watch. Seth could understand why. Perhaps Willis was not being paid by Bentley but doubtless he had to do as he was told.

He switched the whole of his attention back to the two men in front of him. So far, the man on the opposite boardwalk appeared to be completely uninterested in what was going on but Seth knew that he was watching everything, waiting for his companion to make his move before joining in.

Looking directly into the eyes of the man facing him, Seth said softly, 'Are you afraid of this guy Bentley or are you in it just for the money?'

He knew the insult had hit home, saw the man bend forward in a crouch. His right hand struck downward for the Colt. At the same moment, the gunslinger across the street made for his guns. Neither man had time to clear leather before the Colts in Seth's hands spat muzzle flame.

The nearer man slumped forward, knees buckling beneath his weight. For the smallest fraction of a second he knew what had happened. His eyes bulged in their sockets and then rolled upward. He hit the dirt limply, his eyes wide-open, staring vacantly at the sky.

His partner was still standing, struggling to hold life in his limbs. Both guns fell from his nerveless fingers as he put out one hand to clutch at the hitching post. Then all of the life went out of him as he toppled forward against it. Wood splintered beneath him as he pitched on to his face in the street.

Thrusting the Colts back into their holsters, Seth stepped down from the boardwalk. He had only gone a couple of paces when a voice called, 'Hold it right there, mister.'

Glancing up he saw the sheriff striding towards him. Seth's right hand rested lightly on the butt of one of the Colts as he said tightly, 'I hope you ain't thinkin' of arresting me, Sheriff. You saw everythin' that happened. They both drew first.'

'I saw it all,' Willis said gruffly. 'They drew first. I just came to give you a piece of advice. Get the hell out of town right now if you value your life. You've just shot down two o' Herb Bentley's top gunslingers and he'll want your neck in a rope for that.'

'Believe me, Sheriff, once I pick up some grub and ammunition, I'll be out o' here.'

The lawman pointed. 'You'll get food at the store yonder and Clint Forrest will let you have shells. You'll find him at the far end o' the street.'

'Thanks.'

Seth made to walk away but the

lawman stopped him again. 'Take your mount. Once you've got all you need ride out o' town by the north trail and don't head straight back to Jeb's place. It's likely you'll be followed.'

'Thanks again, Sheriff. I sure appreciate that advice.'

By now the two bodies lying in the street had attracted a small crowd. As he swung into the saddle, Seth heard the sheriff shout, 'It's all over, folks. Both o' these men drew first. This man acted in self-defence.'

Ten minutes later, with his saddlebags full of food and boxes of shells, Seth rode out of Cranton, cutting north along a narrow rutted trail. Throwing a swift glance behind him, he noticed that the crowd was still there, larger than before. But in the distance he spotted another group of men. Already they were climbing into the saddle and there was no doubt as to their intention. Bentley had not been long in getting together a band of men to pursue him.

Kicking spurs into the stallion's

flanks, he sent it racing along the trail. The men at his back would all be familiar with the country around Cranton whereas he knew nothing of it. There had undoubtedly been wisdom in Willis's words. If he had ridden back along the way he had come, everyone would know he was staying with Jeb Dawson. Once word of that got back to that mysterious third man, he would immediately know who had killed those two men in the wilderness.

With an effort, he pushed these thoughts from his mind. At the moment he had to concentrate on staying ahead of his pursuers and make certain he didn't lead them to Dawson's spread. Lifting himself in the saddle, he stared behind him.

The first of the riders were just heading out of the town. He judged there were at least half a dozen of them, all pushing their mounts to the limit. Then the rider leading them lifted his right hand and made a signal. Immediately three of the bunch swung away from the others, heading across open country.

Seth smiled grimly to himself. So that was their plan. To split their force and hope to cut him off some distance ahead. Leaning forward in the saddle, he urged more speed from the stallion.

He knew that with every step his mount took he was moving further and further from Jeb's spread. By now, he and his daughter would be wondering what had happened to him. They might even figure that he had decided to pull out and not become involved in their problems. But he couldn't cut back south yet with those men on his trail.

Up ahead, the narrow trail angled sharply to his left, almost doubling back upon itself. Long stands of tall pines stood along either side, their trunks so close together it would be almost impossible to make a way through them. Seth thought fast. Those three men who had broken away from the others just outside of town would know every inch of this country.

By now they would have swung across his path and if he kept to this trail, he would almost certainly find them waiting for him some distance ahead. There was only one way for him to go. Reining up his mount, he looked swiftly about him, searching for some place where it might just be possible to work his way through the trees.

The unmistakable sound of hoofbeats reached him a moment later. Those men at his back were gaining quickly. Making up his mind, he pulled the stallion off the narrow trail towards the pines. For a moment, he thought the animal was going to refuse. Digging spurs into its flanks, he urged it forward.

Rough branches clawed at him as he moved deeper into the forest. In places it seemed impossible for the horse to squeeze through the gap between the rearing trunks. Then, some thirty yards from the track he came upon a small clearing. It was barely wide enough for the stallion to turn round but it was well hidden from the trail.

Tensely, Seth waited. The sound of approaching riders was louder now and after a few seconds he was able to distinguish two sets of hoofbeats. The two groups of his pursuers were meeting up almost exactly opposite the spot where he had halted!

Loud, harsh voices reached him through the screen of trees. A man shouted, 'He must've come this way. There's no other trail he can follow.'

'He never passed us,' called a second.

'Unless he cut across open country to the hills,' suggested another of the riders. 'If he has, there's no way we can trail him into that maze.'

There followed more talk that Seth could not follow. Then they must have reached a decision for a moment later they began moving out, returning along the way they had come.

Seth waited until he could no longer hear the sound of horses, then he pushed the stallion back through the trees. Swinging his mount sharply, he moved along the trail to his right, allowing the horse to pick its own pace for a while.

It was growing dark by the time he spotted the lights in the ranch house windows. As he rode into the small courtyard, the door opened and Belle stepped out on to the veranda. Dropping from the saddle, Seth took down his saddle-bags and slung them over his shoulder.

'What happened?' Belle asked tensely. 'You were gone so long we thought — ' She paused uncertainly, not sure how to go on.

'You thought that maybe I'd decided to leave?' He shook his head. 'I ran into a spot o' trouble in town. Seems there's some *hombre* there who doesn't take too kindly to strangers, particularly if they refuse to work for him.'

'Was he a big man, flashily dressed?' Belle asked, as she walked beside him to the door.

'That's right. I was told his name is Bentley.'

At the door, Belle stood on one side to allow him to go in first. Then she closed and bolted the door. 'Bentley is a dangerous man to cross.'

Lowering the heavy saddle-bags to the floor, Seth straightened. 'I found that out soon enough. He evidently didn't want me walkin' out o' town again. Some Mexican wanted to skewer me with a knife and then I noticed Bentley talkin' to a couple o' gunslingers a few moments later as I stepped out o' the saloon.'

'They tried to kill you?' Belle stared at him, her eyes wide.

'Oh, sure. I guess that's the way Bentley operates. I figure those killers are in the town mortuary by now. Willis saw everythin'. Told me to get what I needed and then ride out o' town by the north trail.'

'I'll get you something to eat,' Belle said, going into the kitchen. 'Then we'll decide what to do.'

3

Shadows In The Night

Seth pushed his empty plate away and sat back in the chair, rolling himself a smoke. The heat from the roaring fire was a pleasant warmth on his shoulders. Belle came in from the kitchen, wiping her hands on her apron.

There was a worried expression on her face as she asked, 'Do you think that attack on you was deliberate? I mean, could it have had any connection with what happened to my father?'

'You reckon this guy Bentley was behind all that and might have figured I was the one who shot those two bushwhackers?'

She nodded.

'It's possible, I suppose,' he acknowledged tightly. 'Two men disappear after going to check on a wounded old man and then a stranger rides into town. it wouldn't take too much to connect the two.'

Finishing his smoke, Seth pushed back his chair and got to his feet.

'Where are you going?' Belle asked anxiously.

'I think I'll take a look around the place before turning in.' Hitching his gunbelt higher around his waist, he went to the door and stepped out on to the veranda. The night was dark and still. Too quiet, he reflected.

He knew the two hired hands were bunked down for the night next to the grain store on the far side of the courtyard. The yellow glow from a paraffin lamp showed through the square window.

Stepping down, he made his way towards the gate, throwing a quick, penetrating glance towards the small corral where the horses were stabled for the night. The full moon threw long black shadows across the ground but nothing moved. Yet he had the uneasy feeling that something was wrong.

Making no sound, he went up to the gate and stared out into the night. The trail from town was little more than a grey blur. As far as he could see, it was empty. Yet the sensation of wrongness persisted. It was something he had experienced several times during the war and each time he had been proved right.

For almost five minutes, he stood there, listening to the various night sounds. He was just on the point of turning away when a faint snicker from one of the horses reached him. For a moment, he could hear nothing to explain the animal's reaction.

Then, above the soughing of the wind in the nearby trees, he picked out the muffled sound of approaching riders. They were approaching slowly and making little noise. Crouching down, he edged back a little way, drawing one of the Colts as he did so. Even in the bright moonlight it was difficult to make out details but then he saw the dark shadows of several men.

He reckoned there were at least a dozen men in the bunch and there was no doubting their intention. Their furtive actions told him that these were not men coming to pay a social call. When the men were some two hundred yards away, one of them lifted a hand. Halting their mounts, they sat there, talking among themselves.

Then a group broke away, circling around to the east, Seth made up his mind at once. He had to warn the others. Bending double, he ran across to the bunkhouse, thrust open the door and then closed it quickly behind him.

'Douse that light.' he called sharply. 'We've got company and it's clear they mean business.'

One of the men immediately extinguished the lamp. 'How many are there?' he rasped harshly.

'About a dozen or so,' Seth told him crisply. 'So far they don't know they've been seen but a group of 'em have cut around to the side. My guess is they may try to fire the grain store and then spook the horses.'

The two men had grabbed their rifles and now took up their stand near the window.

'I'll warn Belle and her father,' Seth said tautly. 'If those critters try to rush the place, they'll have to cross the courtyard. In the moonlight they'll make easy targets.'

Without saying anything more, he ran towards the house. Belle was in the front room as he rushed in. A look of alarm crossed her features at his sudden appearance.

'What is it?' Her voice was little more than a throaty whisper.

'We have visitors. About a dozen of 'em. My guess is they're goin' to hit the spread from two directions. I've alerted the boys in the bunkhouse. You'd better be ready for 'em when they come.'

'I'll be ready.' There was a distinct grimness in her tone now. She crossed the room swiftly, taking down a rifle from the wall. As she came back with it, she paused at the desk near the wall, opened a drawer, and drew out a revolver.

There was no hint of fear on her face as she went to the window. Pressing herself against the wall at one side, she risked a quick look outside.

'Nothing there at the moment,' she remarked.

'The main bunch was about a couple o' hundred yards down the trail when I last saw 'em.'

'This must be more of Bentley's doing,' the girl said harshly, 'although I doubt if he'll be here. He just pays these men to do his killing for him.'

Seth opened his mouth to say something more but at that moment several dark figures appeared at the gate. One of the men shouted, 'We want a word with you, Dawson.'

'Come one step nearer and you won't be talkin' to anyone,' Seth called back.

He saw the man hesitate. Clearly these men were unaware there was anyone else on the spread but Belle and her father.

Then the man yelled again. 'I don't know who you are, mister, but this has nothin' to do with you. This is between us and Jeb Dawson.'

Before he could stop her, Belle called loudly, 'Whatever it is you want you can talk to me. Then all of you get off our land before you collect some lead.'

'This is Clem Henders, Belle. We don't aim to make any trouble. As you know I made your pa a good offer for this spread but he turned it down. I came here tonight hopin' he's seen sense and is now willin' to sell out to me.'

'If you wanted to make my father another offer, Henders, you wouldn't come riding in here at this time of night with a dozen gunmen at your back,' Belle retorted. 'You already know my father's answer. Now I suggest you turn your mounts around and head back to town.'

'All right. If that's the way you want it.' Henders wheeled his mount. Then, without warning, dropped from the saddle as the rest of the men with him did likewise.

In the silver moonlight, Seth saw the men scatter to either side of the gate. Without hesitating, he smashed the window with his gunbutt. The glass was still falling outside as he aimed swiftly, and squeezed the trigger of the Colt twice. Two of the men suddenly lurched as the slugs took them squarely in the chest. Both dropped and lay still.

It was the signal for the others. Keeping his head well down, Seth saw the flashes of muzzle flame. Slugs hit the stout wall beside the window. On the other side, Belle sent several shots into the mass of shadows.

One of the men cried out as he was hit. Through the broken window, more slugs sped into the room and crashed into the far wall. Somewhere, Henders could be heard, calling upon the men to rush the house but with the deadly fire being poured into them none seemed prepared to take the risk.

From the edge of his restricted view,

Seth was able to make out the side of the bunkhouse. The men there were holding their fire ready for any of the attackers who might decide to try for the house. Somewhere at the back of his mind a little thought kept niggling at him.

The men with Henders seemed to be quite content now to remain under cover and pin him and Belle down. Then he recognized what his mind was trying to tell him. That other bunch that had ridden off to the side. What were they doing while he and Belle held off these men?

The answer came to him at once. The grain store! Turning swiftly to Belle, he said sharply, 'Keep me covered.'

'Why? What do you intend to do?'

'That second bunch are heading for the grain store. My guess is they'll try to fire it. And with the wind blowing in this direction, the flames could easily spread to the house.'

Without waiting for any reply, he made for the door, opening it slightly.

Peering through the narrow gap he could just make out the muzzle flashes from close by the main gate. He waited for a moment while he thumbed fresh shells into the Colts, then got his legs under him, pulled open the door, and thrust himself out on to the low veranda.

Keeping his head down, he spun quickly and ran along the wooden slats. Several bullets struck the wall close to his head as he reached the end and vaulted swiftly over the rail. Landing lightly on the other side, he edged quickly along the side of the building, both Colts ready.

The two men in the bunkhouse were still firing at the group near the gate. There was no sign of any other movement. Twenty yards away he made out the large mass of shadow that was the store. At the moment he could see none of the attackers but he knew they weren't far away.

For a split second he debated whether to remain where he was and cover the front of the store, or make a run for the door and wait there. He reached his decision at once. Throwing a swift glance all around him, he darted forward, expecting to hear a gunshot at any moment. But none came.

Evidently, he thought tensely, those other men were taking their time, confident that their companions could keep anyone inside the house pinned down. Crouching down, he waited. He didn't have to wait long.

Less than five minutes later he picked out the sound of approaching riders coming in from the north. There was the snapping of branches as they pushed their way through the small copse along the edge of the spread. They weren't making any attempt to conceal their approach. Clearly they weren't expecting to bump into any trouble.

Pressing himself hard against the inside wall of the shed, Seth narrowed his eyes against the wash of brilliant moonlight that flooded the ground. He heard the horses stop and there was the unmistakable sound of men dismounting.

The first man stepped out of the shadows twenty feet away and stood looking about him. He must have been satisfied that there was no one around for he gave a sharp signal to the others. Three more came out into the open and two of them carried brands in their hands.

Seth smiled grimly to himself. So he had guessed right as to their intentions. After a few moments' talk among themselves, the men came forward in a loose bunch. One of them pointed towards the grain store and gave a quick nod.

Two brief flares sparked in the dimness as the men struck sulphur matches, preparing to light the brands.

Gripping the Colts tightly, Seth called harshly, 'Drop those brands and then shuck your gunbelts.'

He saw the men start, trying to pinpoint his position. Then two of them went for their guns. Both had their weapons clear of leather when Seth fired. The nearest man jerked abruptly on his feet as the heavy slug ploughed into his chest. His arms went up as if he were trying to reach for the sky, both guns going off at the same time. The shots went harmlessly into the air above his head as he fell backward and lay still.

His companion got off one shot that hit the woodwork close to Seth's head. He stood for a moment, swaying on his feet as he struggled to hold life in his body. Then he folded at the knees and went down.

Swiftly, Seth turned his attention to the remaining two gunmen. He saw that both had applied their matches to the brands they held and these were now blazing furiously. One of them drew back his arm as he prepared to throw the brand. He almost made it before Seth's Colts spat blue flame, sending him tumbling backward. The brand fell from his nerveless fingers, falling to the ground a split second before he fell upon it.

Before Seth could turn to face the fourth man, the gunslinger had tossed his lighted brand through the doorway of the store and was running back towards the comparative safety of the trees.

Seth sent a couple of shots after him before turning his attention to the immediate danger. The brand had fallen between two of the large sacks of grain and already both sacks were well alight. Desperately, he yelled to the two men in the bunkhouse but they had already seen the danger and Clint came running towards him, weaving from side to side as bullets tore into the ground around his feet.

'We need water,' Clint said harshly.

Seth shook his head. 'There's no time for that. By the time you get any here this whole place will be on fire. Pull those burning sacks away from the others.'

He pointed to where the flames were licking around the wall just inside the doorway. Ignoring the pain, Seth grasped one of them and heaved it to one side. Smoke was now filling the store, choking him. Gasping and coughing, his eyes streaming, he grabbed another sack and threw it after the first.

After a moment's hesitation, Clint joined in. Wiping away the tears that threatened to blind him, Seth paused and straightened. It was going to be touch and go if they were to save the store. In the direction of the house the sound of gunfire still hammered through the moonlit darkness. Evidently Belle was still giving a good account of herself. Pausing only to wipe the sweat from his face, and take stock of the situation, Seth caught hold of the last of the burning sacks and dragged it to the doorway.

Clint came staggering out and leaned against the doorpost, sucking in deep lungfuls of air. He was coughing violently. Glancing back into the dark interior, he said hoarsely, 'At least we managed to save most of it.' He jerked a thumb towards the three men on the ground. 'And I see you managed to get some of 'em.'

'There was only one left out o' that bunch,' Seth retorted sharply. 'He pulled out and I doubt if he'll come back. In the meantime, I reckon we should help Miss Belle. There are still those others to take care of.'

With Clint behind him, Seth ran back towards the house. Cautiously, he inched his head around the side of the building. Two bodies lay sprawled on the far edge of the courtyard. Evidently, they had attempted to rush the place.

Vaulting over the rail at the end of the veranda, Seth padded towards the door. A slug slammed into the wall near his head and he heard the thin screech of the ricochet.

Before opening the door, he called softly, 'It's me, Belle. Clint and I are comin' in.'

A moment later they were both inside. Belle had extinguished the lamps and the only light in the room was the moonlight filtering through the smashed window. As his eyes became adjusted to the darkness, Seth saw the girl crouched down at the window. Going forward, he dropped down beside her, motioning Clint to the other window.

'I reckon we've got most of 'em,' he said grimly. 'A band of 'em tried to fire the grain store and nearly succeeded.'

'Where are they now?' Belle asked in a taut whisper.

'Three are dead. The fourth got away.'

'And the store?'

'We managed to get all o' the burning sacks o' grain outside where they can't do any harm.' He threw himself down as a fusillade of gunfire crashed through the broken window.

Gritting his teeth, he pressed himself against the wall and lifted his head an inch at a time. The moonlight now touched every corner of the courtyard. Only the two dead gunhawks were visible. Somewhere in the distance a man shouted something but it was impossible for Seth to distinguish any words. However, since the gunfire stopped almost at once Seth reckoned it must have been Henders giving the order.

A few moments later there came the sound of hoofbeats receding swiftly into the distance. Breathing a sigh of relief, Seth pulled himself to his feet and helped Belle to hers.

'I reckon it's over for the time being,' he said soberly. 'I guess they never figured on meetin' such opposition. You sure know how to handle a gun, Belle.'

'In wild country like this you learn at an early age,' she replied, equally soberly. She stood looking out of the window, a serious expression on her face. 'I wonder what they mean to do now. This isn't the end of it. You can be sure they'll be back and the next time they'll bring more men with them.'

Seth knew she was right. Henders and Bentley were men who would never give up. There were always plenty of gunmen around willing to throw in their lot with men such as them.

After reloading the Colts, he thrust them back into their holsters and stared around the room. Apart from the smashed window there didn't seem to be too much damage. Turning to Clint, he said quietly, 'I reckon you should get back to the bunkhouse. Make sure that fire is completely out and then get yourself some sleep.'

'You seem to be pretty sure they won't try to hit us again through the night,' Clint said.

Seth nodded. 'I know these men. They've failed this time and they'll retire to lick their wounds. Henders must've lost close on nine or ten men tonight. He's no fool. It'll take him some time to get more together.'

After Clint had gone, Seth said slowly, 'I've been thinkin'. After what's happened tonight, you've got a big decision to make.'

'Oh? About what?'

'You only have those two hired

hands. They won't be nearly enough against what Henders and Bentley can throw against this place if we were to leave for Condor Peaks. Your father would be totally helpless. And even if we wait until the last possible moment, he certainly would be in no condition to make that journey with us.'

'So what do you suggest? That we stay here and he loses all entitlement to that land?'

Seth spread his hands in a gesture of resignation. 'I only wish there was something I could suggest but it seems that Bentley and Henders hold all of the aces at the moment. Right now, I reckon we should check on your father.'

They found the old man sitting bolt upright in the bed. Somehow, he must have got out for there was a shotgun in his hands. He laid it down beside him as they entered.

'What in tarnation was happening down there?' he demanded.

'Nothin' we couldn't take care of,' Seth said easily.

'Was it Bentley or Henders?'

Seating herself on the edge of the bed, Belle said quietly, 'It was Henders. It seems he's not prepared to wait any longer for you to make up your mind about his offer. He tried to take the ranch by force. Had it not been for Seth here, he might have succeeded.'

'I just did what I had to,' Seth muttered.

'Well, he'd never have lived to take it if he'd taken one step inside that door,' Jeb growled. He inclined his head towards the weapon beside him.

Seth forced a grim smile. 'Unfortunately, his actions present us with a big problem, old-timer.'

'About the two o' you goin' to register my claim?'

'That's right. If I figure that *hombre* rightly, his next step will be to post men all around the ranch to prevent any of us getting out, either for food or help.'

'And there's still Bentley to contend with,' Belle added. 'From what I hear, those two are working together.'

Dawson rubbed a hand across his chin. 'If there was only a way of gettin' word through to the State Marshal in Twin Forks, we might have a chance.'

Belle shook her head. 'That's been tried before when Bentley started running the other small ranchers out of the territory. These two men are too big and powerful and now they have the railroad behind them, I'm afraid we don't count.'

'Then your only hope is to somehow get more men behind you, men fast with a gun who aren't in with either Bentley or Henders.'

'And where would we get them?' Jeb said disconsolately. 'Certainly not in Cranton.'

Sighing, Belle got to her feet. 'Maybe we'll be thinking more clearly after a good night's sleep. Seth reckons they won't come back tonight after losing nearly all of their men.'

The grey light of an early dawn was seeping through the windows when Seth woke the next morning. The sun was not yet up as he stepped out into the yard and built himself a smoke.

Things were looking bad for the girl and her father. He could see no answer to the problem that faced them although he felt sure that Jeb would insist that he and Belle should try to make it to Condor Peaks, even if it meant leaving only him and the two hired hands to defend the ranch.

Finishing the smoke, he ground it into the dirt with his heel. A sudden movement behind him brought him whirling round quickly. The door had opened and Belle stepped outside. She looked as though she had had very little sleep through the night.

'You're up early,' she remarked.

'I was figurin' on takin' a ride out before breakfast,' he told her.

'A ride out?' There was a puzzled frown on her face as she came down the steps to stand beside him. 'Where were you thinking of riding?'

'I've been thinkin' about what happened last night. Henders ain't going to let it rest there. He's got some plan in mind and the sooner we discover what it is, the better. My guess is that he means to bottle us up here by placin' men all around the ranch where they can watch every trail.'

'So you want to check on that?'

There was a strange note in her voice that Seth noticed at once. Somehow, he had the feeling she still did not trust him, was doubtful if he would stay now that things were getting rough.

'That's right. You got any objections?'

He saw her hesitate but only for a fraction of a second. She shook her head. 'No, I think it would be a sensible thing to do. I'll have something ready for you to eat when you get back.' There was another momentary pause and something came into her eyes as she added, 'Take care, Seth. We're in one tight spot and you're the only one who can help us.'

'I'll be careful,' he promised.

Taking the stallion from the corral, he threw on the saddle and tightened the cinch before climbing on to the mount's broad back. Once through the gate, the animal shied a little at the sight of the bodies still lying there. Seth cut away from the main trail and edged the horse into the rough scrubland.

Here the ground was open and desolate where Dawson had clearly not yet got around to clearing it. A quarter of a mile away, however, was a long stand of birch. If there was anyone watching this side of the ranch, he guessed that was the ideal spot for them. As he rode, he kept his glance constantly roving over the territory ahead.

At any moment there might come the sharp bark of a rifle from the dense cover of the undergrowth around the trees. Strangely there was nothing. The silence around him was absolute. And yet he had the feel that something was not quite right.

Reaching the stand of trees, he spotted the narrow track leading deeper into them. It was little more than a game track and hard branches struck him viciously on both sides as he rode forward. The sensation of wrongness grew even stronger in his mind as he progressed, trying to make as little noise as possible.

Not until he reached the wide clearing some fifty yards into the wood did he realize his senses had not let him down. Two men lay face down on the mossy grass. Sliding smoothly from the saddle, he knelt down beside them. One had been shot in the chest while the other had been knifed. Puzzled, he examined them more closely. Both had a thick wad of dollars in their pockets. Clearly they hadn't been killed for their money.

Straightening up, he made to move back to his mount, then halted as a harsh voice called, 'Don't make any move for your guns, mister. There are four rifles trained on you.'

Gritting his teeth, he stood quite still, holding his arms well away from his sides. There came a quiet rustle among the trees and four men stepped into sight covering him with their rifles. All of them wore long black coats that came down to their ankles. A moment later, a fifth man emerged and Seth felt a sudden stab of surprise. This man was an Indian.

Harshly, he said, 'All right, you've got the drop on me. I assume you killed these two men.'

'That's right.' The man Seth assumed to be the leader moved towards him, the rifle rock steady in his hands. 'They tried to jump us as we rode along the trail yonder.'

'And who is it you're workin' for — Bentley or Henders?'

'Never heard o' those names,' the bearded man said. He came closer and stared directly into Seth's face. Then something like surprise and recognition flashed across his swarthy features. 'God Almighty, is it you, Lieutenant? Lieutenant Claybourne?'

'That's my name, but — '

'Guess you don't recognize me,

Lieutenant. Sergeant Hal Durman, Fifth Cavalry.' He lowered his rifle and gave an awkward salute. 'We were all in your platoon at Atlanta when Sherman attacked. Reckon we'd never have got out o' there alive if it hadn't been for you, sir.'

He spun on his heel and called to the others, 'It's Lieutenant Claybourne, boys.'

At his words, the others came forward, lowering their weapons. 'You remember the others, sir? Sam Wellman, Hal Robins and Ken Forde.'

Seth nodded. 'Sure, I remember you. But it's been more than two years and I never expected to find any of you here.'

'We met up almost five months ago in Laredo and decided to head west. That is, all but Grey Shadow here.' He indicated the Indian. 'He's Sioux and a mighty good man to have around. Apart from being able to find food and followin' tracks, he's handy with a knife.'

Durman prodded one of the dead

men with his foot. 'This one never knew what hit him when he tried to pull his guns.'

'Those two men you mentioned, Lieutenant,' put in Forde. 'Why did you figure we might be workin' for them?'

'They're the big men in the town and both are in the business of getting their hands on as much o' the land around here as they can and they don't mind how they do it. At the moment, I'm helping an old-timer and his daughter on a small spread a mile or so away.'

'We were attacked by a dozen of Henders's men last night but we managed to drive 'em off. My guess is that one or the other has posted men around the ranch to prevent anyone ridin' out to get help. That's why I'm here to check things out.'

Durman pursed his lips into a hard, thin line. 'It seems you were right, Lieutenant. These two probably figured we were ridin' in to lend a hand and decided to ambush us.'

'We were just ridin' through mindin'

our own business when we were attacked,' Wellman interjected. 'Seems folk ain't too friendly in these parts.'

'You're right about that,' Seth agreed. 'I don't suppose any o' you men are lookin' for jobs.'

He saw them glance at each other and then Durman said, 'Reckon we might be at that. What kind o'jobs were you thinkin' about?'

'This old timer, Jeb Dawson, only has two hired men and his daughter to help him defend his spread. Seems the railroad wants to take it over and the railroad company has asked Bentley and Henders to help 'em get it. The trouble is, I've got to accompany his daughter to a place called Condor Peaks and once anyone gets to know we've gone, I figure the old man won't have a chance. Right now, he's in bed after havin' a slug taken out of his shoulder.'

'I reckon we might be prepared to help him,' Durman nodded. 'Besides, if it hadn't been for you, none of us would be here now. It's the least we can do for you.'

'Thanks. If you'll follow me, I'll take you to him.'

'Does your offer include Grey Shadow?' Forde asked.

'I don't see why not. Far as I know Dawson ain't got anything against the Sioux.' He waited while the others saddled up, then led the way back through the trees.

4

Night Ride

Belle was standing in the courtyard talking with Clint when Seth rode in with the five men at his back. For a moment she looked startled and surprised as she broke off her conversation.

Stepping down from the saddle, Seth said evenly, 'I've just run into four of the men who were under my command at Atlanta, Belle. The Indian is a Sioux named Grey Shadow who's travellin' with them. They've offered to help you and your father.'

Belle's eyes were hard as she asked, 'Can they be trusted?'

Seth nodded. 'I'll stake my life on it. They're all good men, handy with a gun.' She hesitated for a moment, then made up her mind. 'Bring them in. I'll take your word for them but it will be

104

up to my father as to whether they stay.'

'We understand that, miss,' Durman said soberly.

'We had to kill two men on the way here. From what the lieutenant tells us this place is full o' folk who want to take everything they can get, just like the carpetbaggers back East.'

Belle said nothing to that piece of information and led the way inside and up to the small room at the back. Her father was sitting up in the bed by the window. Seth saw the sudden look of suspicion that crossed the other's grizzled features.

'Who are these men, Belle?' he asked sharply.

Before the girl could answer, Seth said quietly, 'I came upon them in the wood, Jeb, about a couple o' miles away. Like I told Belle, we served together against Sherman when he sacked Atlanta. Seems they owe me a debt of gratitude for gettin' 'em out of there alive.'

Jeb drew his brows together into a

straight line and the suspicious expression remained in his eyes. 'You know anythin' of what's happening here in Cranton?'

As the men shook their heads, he went on, 'The railroad is hopin' to buy up a whole heap o' land around these parts. Most of it belongs to small ranchers like myself. Just to make it look as though everythin' they're doin' is legal, they've got a couple o' men in town, Herb Bentley and Clem Henders to get the land for 'em and they don't particularly care how it's done.'

'These two men have hired an army of gunfighters and the ranchers either sell out to them for hardly anything at all, or they're run off their spreads,' Belle put in. 'Then Bentley and Henders make a big profit sellin' it to the railroad.'

'Seems to me they're even worse than those carpetbaggers,' Forde muttered.

'Then I take it you don't agree with what they're doin',' Jeb said, eyeing each man in turn.

106

'Except for Grey Shadow, we all fought in the Confederate Army hopin' to preserve the ways of the South,' Durman replied with a note of pride in his voice. 'Those days are gone now but believe me, this isn't what we fought for.'

Dawson switched his glance to Seth. 'This man saved my life out in the Badlands. I guess if he says you're all right, I'll accept his judgement, I can't pay much but you'll get grub and a place to sleep.'

'Does that include our friend here?' Durman inclined his head towards the Indian standing silently just inside the doorway, his arms folded across his chest.

'I've got no quarrel with the Sioux,' Dawson told him.

'Then I guess you're hired,' Seth said.

'I'll make some more food,' Belle said, as she led them back down the stairs. 'Then I'd like to talk to you, Seth.'

After they had eaten and the five men had taken their belongings to the bunkhouse, Seth went over to the corral where Belle stood waiting. As he rolled a smoke, she said anxiously, 'I don't wish to question your word or judgement, but are you absolutely certain we can trust these men?'

'Like I said, I'd trust all of these men with my life. It may not be easy for you to understand but in war you soon get to know those men you can rely on when things get really rough. I'll admit I know nothin' at all about the Indian but at this moment you need all of the men you can get.'

'And if you and I were to leave for Condor Peaks, they'll help my father to defend the ranch?'

Seth gave an emphatic nod. 'I'm absolutely sure of it,' he assured her.

She still did not appear to be entirely convinced but she nodded before making her way back towards the house. Over her shoulder, she called, 'We'll talk with my father this afternoon. I think we should prepare to leave as soon as possible.'

* * *

By the time it was growing dark they had almost completed their preparations. Standing beside the bed, Seth took the deeds that Dawson handed to him. 'Take care o' these' Jeb said thickly. 'They're about all I have left and I figure there are plenty o' men out there willin' to do anythin' to get their hands on 'em.'

Seth thrust them inside his jacket. 'I'll get these through to the registry office at Condor Peaks,' he promised, 'though I still don't like the idea of Belle comin'. It's a long and dangerous trail and not one for a woman.'

'You won't get me to change my mind,' Belle said from the other side of the bed. 'I'm coming and that's all there is to it.'

Seth gave her a direct stare. 'You still don't really trust me, do you?'

'That's something I've learned living here,' she replied tautly. 'I trust no one except my father.'

'Evidently he trusts me,' Seth retorted.

The girl bit her lower lip and did not reply. Glancing back to the man in the bed, Seth changed the subject. 'The way I see it, Henders and the others will have staked out men to watch every way out o' here. I doubt if they'll attack again in the near future but at least you have help now.'

Dawson pushed himself up on the pillows. 'Once that pesky doctor lets me get on my feet, I'll be headin' that way to join you. This place don't mean much to me now. I reckon I can make a better life at Condor Peaks.'

'You're thinking about building a place out there?' There was surprise in Belle's voice. 'You never mentioned this before.'

'I've been thinkin' about it for a long time. That's good country yonder and there ain't much good you can say about Cranton.'

'Guess that'll be your decision,' Seth said, shrugging his shoulders, 'but right now, we have to think of a way of gettin' out of here without bein' seen by any o' Henders's men.'

In spite of the pain in his shoulder, Dawson forced a smile. 'I've also been thinkin' about that. I've had a talk with Grey Shadow. He'll go with you until you're out in open country. He can scout ahead for any trouble and take care of it in his own way.'

After a moment's deliberation, Seth gave a nod of agreement. The Sioux could move as silently as a cat and, while a gunshot might alert any other men in the vicinity, his knife made no sound at all.

The moon, just past full, was rising over the hills to the east when they saddled up their mounts and prepared to move out. Grey Shadow was a dark shape a few feet away. Unlike Belle and Seth, he had no mount but stood ready to move on foot beside them. Swinging up into the saddle, Seth waited for Belle to mount, every nerve alert as he scanned the dark shadows around them. Then they rode together, through the gate and on to the narrow track. Here, they only progressed for a couple of yards before swinging away into the brush.

All the way, Seth had the feel of eyes watching their every move. Twenty yards into the undergrowth, Grey Shadow motioned for them to halt. A moment later, he had drifted away into the moonlit dimness making no sound as he melted into the background.

Seth waited tensely, his right hand close to the Colt at his waist. Around them, the silence seemed absolute.

Five minutes passed and then another five. Then a sudden movement alerted him to the Indian's return.

'Three men at the bottom of the hill yonder.' Grey Shadow raised an arm and pointed. 'They are no longer any danger to you. Now we must take that path through the trees.'

Making as little noise as possible they

followed the Sioux as he led them towards the distant hill. Around them, the night seemed full of menace. At any moment, Seth expected to hear the sharp bark of a rifle and feel the impact of a bullet.

But it seemed that Grey Shadow was right. Nothing happened and a few moments later he saw why. Three bodies lay in the thick brash where Grey Shadow had hauled them off the narrow track. There were the remains of a small fire close by but no sign of any horses.

'Their mounts must've bolted just after you left,' Seth observed. 'Once they get back into town without their riders, Headers will know that somethin' has happened.' He turned in the saddle to face Belle. 'I reckon we have to get as far away from here as possible before someone comes lookin' for these men.'

'Once you reach the hills you should be safe,' Grey Shadow said.

Seth was not so sure. The fact that

three of Headers's men had been killed tonight would make him think. How much the man knew about Dawson's deeds Seth didn't know. But it wouldn't be too difficult to figure out what was happening — that someone was heading for Condor Peaks to file those documents. Once that happened, there would be men on their trail.

Giving the Indian a wave of farewell, they set off at a brisk gallop, taking the narrow game trail that led over the hills. Overhead, the sky was completely clear with the moon beginning to rise higher towards the east.

★ ★ ★

The Golden Horseshoe was, by far, the largest saloon in Cranton and the one where Herb Bentley was most likely to be found at that time of the evening. He was seated in the corner furthest from the door with his back to the wall.

Not only did this allow him to keep a sharp eye on everything, it also meant that no one could take him unawares and try to shoot him in the back. Three other men were seated at the table with him: Clem Henders at his right hand with Reuben Curtis, the town mayor, directly opposite him and Judge Harold Corday on his left.

All three of Bentley's companions were watching him with some apprehension, wondering why he had called them together. It was evident that Bentley was in a foul mood as he yelled for more whiskey to be brought to the table.

Once the bottle was placed in front of him, he poured out some of the liquor into their glasses. Then, breaking the uncomfortable silence, he said sharply, 'Well, what are we goin' to do about this man, Dawson? I suppose he still refuses to sell out.'

Henders nodded. 'He's got some hired gunslinger workin' for him. Whoever he is, he's good with a gun. I lost several of my men when we hit them the other night.'

'So I've heard.' Bentley scrutinized each of the others in turn before asking, 'Do any of you know anythin' about him. Who he is? Where he's from?'

All three shook their heads.

'What's worryin' you, Herb?' The judge fiddled nervously with his fingers. 'He's only one man. With all the gunslicks you have workin' for you, you can take him any time you like.'

Bentley tossed half of his whiskey down in a single gulp, his face twisted into a scowl. 'Unfortunately, it ain't quite as easy as that, Judge. The railroad are mighty keen that everythin' is done accordin' to the law. So far, this *hombre* hasn't done anythin' against the law.'

'Except help to kill a number o' my men,' Henders snapped viciously.

Bentley's lips were twisted into a faint sneer as he retorted, 'And whose fault was that? I warned you that you were courtin' trouble hittin' Dawson's spread. That was a stupid thing to do.'

Colour darkened the cattleman's

features and for an instant a sharp retort rose to his lips. With an effort, he forced it down. 'All right.' he grated 'So what do you suggest we do? Let these small ranchers ride roughshod over everythin' we're tryin' to do? I've already heard rumours that the railroad might decide to approach the ranches directly. If they do that, they may get much o' the land they want a sight more cheaply than by dealin' with us.'

Pouring more drink into his glass, Bentley nodded his head. 'That's why this has got to be done quickly and carefully, otherwise we might find that the railroad will change their plans. They're getting' pretty impatient and if they don't get that land somehow they may even pull out and Cranton will become just another frontier backwater town.'

'Then you've got a plan?' Curtis asked, leaning forward.

'You're the mayor o' this town,' Bentley continued. There was a crafty look in his eyes. 'The first thing you do is tell Willis to get out there and find out exactly what's goin' on.' He suddenly swung his gaze to Henders. 'Accordin' to you, several o' your men haven't returned from keeping watch on that spread. My guess is they've either run out on you, or they've been spotted and killed.'

'If the latter is the case, then you can bring a charge o' murder against Dawson and his hired gunhawk,' said Curtis, downing the remainder of his drink. 'I presume those men had orders not to stray on to Dawson's land while they were keepin' a watch on the place.'

'They had.'

'So they were shot while on the open range,' interjected Corday. 'But as judge here, I'd suggest that if you want to bring a charge of murder it might be better if we got a state marshal and let him take it from there. That way we'd keep in with the railroad and show everyone we're keepin' strictly to the letter o' the law.'

'Why should we do that?' demanded

Bentley harshly. 'We've got you here to preside over a court o' law. Everything will be done in a proper and legal fashion. I'm sure that once the jury hear all o' the evidence they'll reach the right verdict.'

He lifted a hand to indicate that the discussion was finished. Glancing at the mayor, he said thinly, 'Now you just go and find Sheriff Willis and tell him to ride out and bring Dawson and his hired killer in for questioning.'

Curtis scraped back his chair and got slowly to his feet. 'I still don't like it,' he muttered.

'You don't have to like it,' Bentley snapped. 'We run this town and we run it the way we want it.' He watched as Curtis turned and left the saloon. Then he said in a low voice, 'I didn't want him to hear any o' this but we've got to move fast. What we're goin' to tell you now, Judge, you tell no one else. You got that?'

Corday nodded.

'We're not interested in Dawson's

spread,' Henders said, keeping his voice down so that he could not be overheard. 'We're after somethin' much bigger than that.'

'Somethin' bigger?' Corday looked mystified.

'That's right. Dawson has the deeds to a big stretch o' land some hundred miles to the north-east. Seems he got it before the war started but he ain't registered it yet.'

Corday ran a finger down his cheek. 'You know where this land is?'

'Sure we know,' Henders went on. 'Two o' my boys and myself were in Twin Forks a few days ago and we followed him into the bank there. Seems he had the deeds stached away in some deposit box. We trailed him across the Badlands where we held him up.'

'So you've got these deeds?' Corday's interest quickened.

'Unfortunately, we had to shoot him when he opened up on us. We searched every place but there was no sign of 'em. I sent my boys back that night to make sure he was dead and make another search.'

'And what happened?'

'Neither of my boys came back.'

Corday leaned back in his chair, a disappointed expression on his flabby features. 'So you're sayin' that your boys found the deeds and they've lit out with 'em?'

'No, I'm sayin' that this was when Dawson met up with this gunfighter and he killed 'em. Dawson still has those deeds and somehow he has to get to Condor Peaks before the time runs out and that land reverts back to the government.'

'Well, word is that Dawson's in no fit condition to go anywhere. Reckon you don't have to worry none about him gettin' to Condor Peaks and registerin' his claim.'

Bentley took out a cigar from his breast pocket and lit it, blowing smoke into the air. 'If I could be sure o' that, I might sleep better at night.'

'You got somethin' else on your mind?' Corday signalled to the bartender and Bentley remained silent as more whiskey was brought and the man had returned to his place behind the counter.

Leaning forward a little, Bentley said softly, 'Dawson's no fool. He knows there's no time to waste and his daughter can't go in his place. My guess is that he might just be desperate enough to trust this gunman to take those deeds and register 'em in his name.'

Compressing his lips into a tight line, Corday sat for a moment, turning that thought over in his mind. 'I suppose that could be possible. Whether the authorities would regard it as fraud is difficult to tell, someone passin' himself off as somebody else, but — '

He broke off sharply as the saloon doors were thrust open and someone came in, Henders swung round in his chair as the man came towards them.

'Reno! What the hell are you doin'

here? I told you to keep a watch on Dawson's spread.'

The Mexican thinned back his lips. 'I was there, Señor Henders. I had men all around the ranch like you ordered.'

'So why are you here?'

'Sanchez and I were on the ridge north of the ranch when we saw three people leave, two on horseback, the other on foot. They headed away from us towards where three of the others were keeping watch so we didn't go after them.'

Henders slammed his fist down on the table spilling most of his drink. 'Goddamnit! I gave orders that no one was to leave. Why didn't you stop them?'

Reno shrugged. 'We knew they'd be spotted by the others and it may have been a ruse to draw us away from our position.'

'Were you able to identify any of the men you saw?' Bentley asked calmly.

'Not with certainty, *señor*. The one on foot I am fairly sure was an Indian and one of the riders could have been a woman.'

'Then it's possible that Dawson has ridden out after all,' Corday muttered, glancing from Henders to Bentley. 'I'd say that puts matters in a different light.'

'It's still possible they ran into my men,' Henders replied, but there was little conviction in his tone. 'If they have they're either dead or my boys will soon be bringin' them into town.'

Bentley stubbed out his cigar and rubbed the ash from his fingers. He could see all of the plans they had made slipping through their fingers but he forced himself to think calmly and logically.

At last he said tautly, 'We have to be absolutely certain. I reckon we have to accept the possibility that Dawson, or that gunslinger, is headin' for Condor Peaks.' He twisted his lips into a faint smile. 'But it's a long way there and anythin' can happen on the way.'

Swinging on Henders, he said smoothly,

'Can you get some men together in a hurry. It shouldn't take too long to overtake these three and — '

'Two, señor.' Reno spoke up. 'We saw the Indian return less than half an hour later. He was alone.'

Henders got to his feet, his mouth twisted into an angry grimace. 'Get three men, Reno, and you go with them. I want those two stopped and I don't care how you do it. Do you understand?'

'Perfectly, Señor Henders.' Reno nodded.

'And once it's done, you bring back those deeds to me. If you fail this time, you'll answer for it.'

★ ★ ★

They rode swiftly through the night and the first grey light of dawn found them beside a wide river where they halted, allowing the mounts to drink their fill. Sitting on the lush grass by the riverbank, Belle said suddenly, 'You're

125

still angry at me for insisting on coming with you, aren't you, Seth?'

For a few moments, he said nothing, chewing on the food they had brought with them. Finally, he replied, 'There's bad country almost all the way to this place your father spoke of. I don't think it's a trail for a woman to take.'

'You seem to be more afraid for me than you are for yourself.'

'I suppose I am.'

'Then you needn't be. And I assure you I won't slow you down. I learned to ride before I was five years old — and how to handle a gun.'

Seth's month twisted into a wry smile. 'And have you ever had to kill a man?'

Belle's retort was sharp. 'You're forgetting I killed three of those men who attacked the ranch. Long ago I discovered that you either kill or be killed.'

Seth suddenly found himself regarding her with a new respect. For the moment, he had forgotten about that

126

night. There was a certain hardness about her that he had not recognized before.

Finishing their meal, they climbed back into the saddle. After fording the river, they rode for most of the morning through dense timberland where the trees grew so thickly together it was almost impossible to find a way through them. It was not until the sun had climbed to its zenith that they came out of the cooling shade. In front of them stretched a wide region of scrubland dotted here and there with spiky cactus, Spanish Sword and a few straggling bushes.

Squinting against the vicious glare of sunlight, Seth reined up his mount and motioned to the girl to do likewise. As he built himself a smoke, he said, 'I reckon we're safe here for a while. We'd better get some sleep before tackling that wasteland.'

'Oughtn't we to push on for another couple of hours?' Belle asked.

Seth shook his head emphatically.

'Not unless you want to be roasted alive in the heat out there. Besides, the horses are tired. They need to be fresh when we start out to cross yonder. My guess is we'll have to ride more'n twenty miles before we reach those hills on the other side.'

He pointed to where a dusty, purple haze marked the far boundary. Making no further protest, Belle stretched herself out on the grassy bank and closed her eyes. Seth sat for a while, listening intently to the sounds all around him.

He had deliberately omitted to tell her what was on his mind, that it would not be long before Headers and Bentley realized that they had slipped through the cordon set up around the ranch. Once that happened, they could expect to have men on their trail.

After a while, he lay down, tipped his hat over his eyes and within minutes, he was asleep. When he opened his eyes again it was to find Belle already awake. Judging by the position of the sun, winking intermittently through the swaying branches, it was late in the afternoon.

Getting to his feet, he said quietly, 'We'd better start out again if you feel up to it.'

'I'm ready when you are.' There was still a stiffness in her voice.

'Good. Then we'll have something to eat, fill our canteens, and be on our way. We should lose some of this heat in a little while.'

The meal was one of silences. Seth knew she was still unsure of him and it was going to take a lot to rid her mind of the possibility that he would claim this piece of territory for himself.

The blazing disc of the sun was now perceptibly lowering westward when they put their mounts to the downgrade and set out across the arid waste that confronted them. Some of the noon heat, however, was still in the unmoving air, reflected from the ground all around them.

Every few minutes, Seth would turn

in the saddle and scan the terrain at their backs. The nagging suspicion that, very soon, there would be gunmen on their trail, refused to go away. But with evening fast approaching, the desert behind them remained clear of any dust that would have shown the presence of riders pursing them.

They rode north as quickly as possible in the endlessly shifting sand, seldom speaking. Seth was glad when night came and he was able to suggest they stop and make camp. He would have preferred to ride on through the night and had he been alone he would certainly have done so but it was plain that not only the girl, but the horses were tiring.

Sliding from the saddle, he went forward and helped Belle from hers, relieved that she did not push him away as he had expected.

As she seated herself on the soft ground, she asked in a low voice, 'You seem to be expecting trouble. I noticed how you kept watching over your shoulder all the time we were riding.'

He forced a grim smile. 'In circumstances like these one has to be prepared for anythin'.'

Turning his head, he stared into the deepening darkness behind them. 'I'm afraid we daren't light a fire even if there was plenty of dry brush. Out here, in this flat country, it would be seen for miles.'

She said nothing but ate the food he had given her, obviously engrossed in her own thoughts. Not until she had finished and washed it down with a little of their water, did she say, 'Just what kind of a man are you, Seth? What is it you're looking for?'

Seth shrugged. Her face was a pale blur and he knew she was watching him closely. 'I'm lookin' for the same as most folk, I guess. I've had enough of war. All I want is a place where I can settle down.'

'And you think you'll find it around here?'

'There's certainly nothin' for me to

go back east for. The Yankees have taken everythin' they could lay their hands on. I reckoned the only thing left for me was to ride west.'

'Even that hasn't brought what you wanted, has it? You've had to kill men just to stay alive.'

'I guess you're right. Sometimes I wonder if there'll ever be an end to it.' Getting to his feet, he said, 'I reckon you should try to get some sleep. We still have a long ways ahead of us and tomorrow will be no different from today.'

'Aren't you going to get some rest?'

'I'll keep watch for a few hours. Just in case anyone is followin' us.'

★ ★ ★

It was early dusk when Sheriff Willis rode into the courtyard of the small spread. His earlier meeting with the mayor had been heated. He did not take too kindly at being ordered around. His job was simply to attempt to keep law and order in Cranton and not to run errands for anyone.

As far as he was aware, Jeb Dawson had been well within the law to defend his property against those men Henders had sent out. As for this gunfighter Dawson was supposed to have hired, he knew nothing against the man.

Unsure of the kind of welcome he would get here, he approached the front door cautiously. Dawson would be prepared for anything after all that had happened and he didn't want a bullet in the chest before he could explain his presence.

The door opened when he was still twenty yards away and someone stepped out. The man had a rifle in his hands and Willis experienced a faint shock of surprise. The other was someone he didn't recognize, a man he had never seen before.

'What do you want here, Sheriff?' the man called, keeping the rifle trained on Willis.

Keeping his hands well away from his

sides, Willis said loudly, 'I just want a word with Jeb Dawson.'

'Are there any more men with you?'

'No. I'm alone.' Feeling distinctly uneasy, Willis approached the other. 'Now do I get to talk with Jeb, or not?'

After a brief pause, the other said, 'I guess you'd better come inside.' He stood on one side and Willis brushed past him into the parlour. Dawson was seated in a large armchair close to the fire, his right shoulder bandaged.

'All right, Willis,' he said, 'what is it you want to see me about?' Although his voice was weak there was an iron note of defiance in it.

'The mayor asked me to call in and check that everythin' is all right. I heard you had some trouble a few nights ago.'

'Nothin' we couldn't handle, Sheriff.'

Willis lifted his gaze from the man in front of him and threw a swift, appraising glance through the wide window. 'I see you have more horses corralled yonder,' he observed.

'I figured I might need more men to

help. Just in the event that Bentley or Henders might still have ideas about tryin' to run me off the spread.'

'And what does your daughter think about that? I don't see her around — or that gunslinger who was here the last time I came.'

Dawson narrowed his eyes as he stared up at the lawman. 'I reckon my daughter has a mind of her own, Sheriff. What she does is no business o' yours.'

For a moment, Willis stood irresolute, his lips pressed into a tight, hard line, and then gave a brief, jerky nod. 'All right, Jeb, I guess I can let Mayor Curtis know that you're on the mend.' Turning on his heel he let himself out.

On the veranda, he stood for a moment. From what he could see, Dawson had somehow hired several more men. Furthermore, it was quite clear that neither Belle Dawson nor that gunman was anywhere on the spread. What Curtis would make of that, he didn't know. Climbing into the saddle, he rode out through the gates, aware that eyes were watching his every move.

* * *

Less than two hours later, after listening to what Willis had to say, Curtis took his horse and trap out to Bentley's spread up in the hills overlooking Cranton. The house was built in the old Colonial style and had somehow escaped the ravages of the recent war.

Just as he entered the long drive, two men armed with rifles stepped out of the bushes on either side. Although Curtis had encountered this before he still felt a sharp stab of anger. He had the impression that, although Bentley was one of the two most influential men in town, he was still obsessed with this security.

In the darkness, he recognized neither of the two men as he called angrily. 'This is Mayor Curtis. I have to speak to Herb Bentley.'

One of the men stepped forward, his rifle still trained on Curtis. His companion said abruptly, 'It's the mayor all right. Let him pass.'

Lowering his weapon, the man waved him on without a word. Gritting his teeth to keep his anger in check, Curtis lashed the horse with his whip, sending it leaping forward. Inwardly, he thought, *It's about time that people around here get to know my position in this town.*

The sense of resentment was still simmering within him as he pulled up at the front door and climbed out of the trap. Lights were streaming through the lower windows. A moment later the door opened and Bentley came out. 'You want to see me, Curtis?' he asked bluntly.

'Yes, I have some important information I think you want to hear.'

Bentley drew deeply on his cigar. 'All right, what is it?'

'I've just heard from Sheriff Willis. It seems that Dawson has hired more men. Also that neither his daughter, nor that gunslinger, is there at the ranch.'

Bentley nodded. 'I appreciate this. Now if you'll excuse me, I have an important meeting goin' on inside. This information will be very useful to me, Curtis. You've done well. I'll take over from here.'

Turning on his heel he went back inside, closing the door behind him.

Curtis went back to the buggy, a white-hot fury boiling away inside him. He felt like going back into the house and telling Bentley that he no longer wanted this job as mayor, that he could give it to someone else. He was fed up with being treated like a lackey, taking orders from Bentley and Henders. Even as the thought crossed his mind, however, he knew it would do no good. Those two men were the real power here in Cranton. There was nothing to prevent either of them getting the bank to foreclose on the loan he'd taken out on his house and land. If that happened, it would certainly be the finish of him.

Pulling himself back into the trap, he seized the whip and lashed it savagely across the horse's back, sending it running back along the trail into town.

Inside the house, Bentley went back into the parlour, closing the door behind him. There were three men seated around the table, all of them important men with the railroad.

Seating himself at the head of the table, he spread his hands apologetically. 'Sorry about that intrusion, gentlemen,' he said smoothly. 'The mayor rode out to give me some information. I'm sure it could've waited until the morning but I guess you know how these officials are. Everything, no matter how trivial, assumes great importance in their minds. However, let's get back to business. I gather you're all in agreement that the railroad passes, not only through Cranton, but also further north.'

Cy Hewitt, the man nearest to him, gave a brief nod. 'That's correct but only if we can resolve this matter of the land across which the railroad will be built.'

At the other side of the table Rufus Conway chipped in, 'From what we understand, there are still a number of ranchers who've declined to sell to you in spite of everything you've done to convince them. Furthermore, we have the problem of this man Dawson who apparently has the deeds to the piece of territory north of here at Condor Peaks. What's happening about him?'

Bentley placed his hands flat on the table in front of him. 'I can assure you that there'll be no trouble on that particular score. Those deeds Dawson has will run out in a few days unless he can register them in person at Condor Peaks.'

'And you're telling us that this won't be the case?' Jed Forbes, the third man, interrupted.

'Unfortunately, Dawson was shot in the shoulder some time ago on his way here from Twin Forks. He's in absolutely no condition to travel, certainly not the hundred miles to Condor Peaks.'

Bentley leaned back in his chair and placed his fingertips together, eyeing each man in turn. He wasn't completely sure he had convinced them but he had no intention of telling them how the girl and that gunhawk were at that moment on their way to Condor Peaks with the deeds. Inwardly, he was certain that Reno and the other men would overtake them long before they reached their destination.

5

Killer Among The Rocks

The grey light of early dawn was spreading across the ground when Seth woke. Turning his head, he saw that Belle was awake, seated some distance away on a small rise, watching the trail along the way they had come the day before. Some time during the early morning, she had woken and insisted on keeping watch while he got some rest.

She looked pale and drawn and there were dark smudges under her eyes as she glanced round at him.

'Why didn't you wake me earlier?' he demanded.

'You must have been awake for most of the night.'

'Until we get to Condor Peaks I intend to do my share,' she told him.

There was no emotion in her voice.

Getting to his feet, he scanned the horizon in every direction. It seemed unlikely that Bentley and the others were not aware that they had left the spread, nor that nothing would be done to stop them reaching their destination.

The thought not only puzzled him. It worried him too. Either any pursuer had also stopped to rest through the night — or they had guessed which route he and the girl would take and decided to circle around them. If that was the case, they could expect trouble once they reached the hills in the distance.

He voiced his fears to Belle, noticed the faint gust of expression that crossed her face. Then she shrugged her shoulders. 'If they try that, we'll be ready for them.' Picking up the rifle that lay beside her within easy reach, she stood up and walked to her mount, thrusting the weapon inside its sheath.

By the time they had eaten a frugal meal and saddled the horses there was a deep red glow to the east and a little while later the sun came up. The morning passed slowly, each individual hour dragging itself out in an agony of heat and thirst. A wind had got up, throwing stinging grains of sand into their faces.

Now they were entering a region of high sandstone bluffs where they were forced to wend their way between tall red ridges that towered twenty or thirty feet above them. By noon, with the sun poised at its zenith, they were forced to halt in the shadow of one of these buttes. Mopping the sweat from his face, Seth dropped from the saddle and moved back a few paces. Staring through red-rimmed eyes, he scanned the terrain to the south.

At first, he could make out nothing in the stabbing sunglare. Then, tensely, he focused his gaze on one particular spot. He had not been mistaken! Swiftly, he called Belle to his side and pointed.

'It's just as I figured,' he uttered grimly. 'We're bein' followed.'

Screwing up her eyes, Belle held up a hand to shield her face from the glare. Seth heard her harsh intake of breath as she made out the small dust cloud.

It was several miles away but it was evident the riders were spurring their mounts to the limit.

'I reckon it'll take 'em about an hour to get here.' Seth rubbed a hand across his forehead where the sweat and irritating sand made his flesh itch. Turning swiftly, he threw a quick, questing glance towards the north. 'The horses are tired. Somehow I doubt if we can reach those hills in time to find some place to hide.'

'Then we'll have to fight it out with them here.' The defiant note was back in the girl's voice. 'We've no other choice.'

'That would be foolish. We've no idea how many men there are in that bunch. Sure, we could do that and mebbe take some of 'em with us. Sometimes caution is the best policy. My guess is they haven't seen us yet and this wind is coverin' our tracks almost as soon as we make 'em.'

'You're saying there's a chance they might ride right past us?'

'I'm sayin' it's the only chance we've got. I know that means that when we go on they'll be somewhere ahead of us but at least we'll be ready for 'em.'

Belle still appeared dubious. Seth knew she was anxious to go on as quickly as possible. There were still more than seventy miles to cover before they reached their destination and time was running out. If these men somehow realized they had missed them somewhere along the trail and decided to lie in wait for them, proceeding with the necessary caution would slow them down even further.

Taking the two horses, he led them further into the deep shadow cast by the butte. He knew the big risk they were taking. So long as those riders kept to their trail they would pass more than two hundred yards from where he and the girl were concealed. But if they

146

should deviate from it and swing around to the north of the line of buttes they would surely be discovered.

To the girl, he said sharply, 'Stay right here. I'm goin' up there to keep an eye on 'em.'

'Be careful they don't see you,' she said warningly.

'I will.' The smooth side of the butte was more difficult to negotiate than he had expected. Several times, he almost lost his footing as his boots slipped on the sandstone. Slowly, inch by inch, he pulled himself up.

Finally, he reached a narrow ledge that ran along the top. Crouching down, he lifted his head slowly, squinting into the blazing sunlight. The men were much closer now, lashing their mounts cruelly as they forced them on. He made out five of them and instantly recognized the leader as the Mexican, Reno, he had encountered before. There was now no doubt in his mind that these were Henders's men.

All of the riders had their heads low

against the whirling sand lifted by the wind. Noticing this, Seth experienced a sense of relief. Three of them had bandannas tied across the lower half of their faces with only their eyes showing. From the speed they were travelling it seemed unlikely that any of them was watching the terrain to either side.

For several minutes he watched their progress until he was satisfied the band did not intend to change their direction. Edging back, he lowered himself carefully down the rock, sliding the last couple of yards.

Belle was standing with her back to the butte and he noticed she was holding both Colts in her hands. She threw him a questioning glance as he got to his feet and went to join her.

'We're in luck. They're not botherin' to watch the trail on either side. This wind may be a nuisance but at the moment it seems to be on our side.'

Now all they could do was wait tensely as the minutes dragged by. They could hear little. Their pursuers rode in silence and in the soft sand the horses made little sound. Finally, Seth moved a short distance from the butte and glanced towards the north. Then he let his breath go in a long sigh of relief.

The gang was almost half a mile away and still spurring their mounts to the utmost limit. 'We're safe for the moment but unfortunately we'll have to watch every inch of the way from now on.'

They rested throughout the long afternoon although Seth could see that Belle was fretting at the delay. Even in the black shadow of the butte the heat was stifling but fortunately they were out of the full fury of the wind. Shortly before the colours of the sunset faded completely, the weather began to change.

The air grew perceptibly cooler and now, instead of blowing steadily, the wind came in savage gusts from the north-west. A few stars began to show but these were soon blotted out by dark clouds that scurried across the heavens, driven on by the gale.

Leaning towards the girl, Seth said loudly, 'We'll soon have to find shelter. Now that the wind has changed direction, there's very little here and by the look of those thunderheads this storm is goin' to be a real beauty.'

'There doesn't seem to be much cover around here,' she agreed, raising her voice to make herself heard above the shrieking of the wind.

Seth pointed into the encroaching darkness. 'There's somethin' yonder. Looks like a jumble o' rocks. It might not be much but it'll be better than out here.'

Going to where the horses were waiting patiently, they swung up into the saddle and started out into the gusting wind. Minutes later the rain began in earnest, large drops that soaked into their clothing. Lightning flashed across the sky followed by the sonorous rumbles of thunder. By the time they reached the rocks they were completely drenched.

Some fifty yards into the dark mass of rock Seth spotted a deep recess that looked wide enough to take them and the horses. Gratefully, they slid from the saddle and led their mounts inside. There was barely enough room for them to turn round but at least they were out of the torrential rain and howling wind.

As they were soon to discover, however, they were not the only occupants of this shelter. As Belle made her way around her mount she suddenly uttered a loud cry of pain. Swiftly, Seth was beside her. He picked out the ominous rattle a few seconds later.

Instinctively, he drew his Colt and fired almost without taking aim. The rattler dropped from the narrow ledge where it had been coiled.

'Did it bite you?' he asked anxiously. In the darkness he just made out the nod of her head.

'Damn.' He muttered the word under his breath. Aloud, he said tautly, 'I'll

151

have to try to get the poison out. I'm afraid this is goin' to hurt.'

Bending as low as possible in the confined space, he took out his box of sulphur matches and struck one as she raised her long riding skirt. In the faint light it was just possible to make out where the cruel fangs had pierced the flesh of her leg, just below the knee.

Reaching up to his saddle, he withdrew the small whip and wound it tightly around her leg above the marks. 'Hopefully that tourniquet will prevent the poison from spreading until I can get it all out,' he said. 'Do you reckon you can hold these for me?' He held up the box of matches.

She took them from him and he noticed her hand was shaking.

'Sit down on that ledge and strike one for me.' In the flickering light he took out the small flask of whiskey, uncorked it, and ran the liquid over the blade of his hunting knife. 'This is the best I can do until we get you to a doctor.'

He gave her the flask. 'Drink some of that. It may help to numb the pain.'

'What are you going to do?' There was a distinct tremor in her voice as she asked the question.

'Only one thing I can do. I'll have to suck out the poison. Otherwise, I'm afraid you'll be dead in a very short time.' He knew it sounded callous but he wanted to evoke a shock response.

'Are you ready?'

'Yes. Go ahead with what you have to do.'

'Just strike another match and hold it down here.' As she did so, he drew the honed blade across the flesh where the mark of the fangs showed in the dim radiance. He heard her sharp intake of breath but she did not cry out. Waiting a few seconds for the blood to flow, he bent and applied his lips to the flesh, sucking out the blood and spitting it into the rocks nearby. Not until he figured that all of the poison was out of the wound did he stop.

'I'm goin' to have to tear a strip of

your petticoat,' he told her. 'I reckon I got most, if not all, of the poison out but I'll have to bandage it up. Then we'll have to find some town where there might be a doctor.'

Within moments he had cut a strip of linen from the bottom of her petticoat and had wound it tightly around the wound. It was still bleeding a little but not as profusely as before once he removed the leather tourniquet. Inwardly, he felt a new admiration for her. Any other woman, he told himself, would have fainted and she had uttered scarcely a sound.

Moving along towards his saddle-bag, he rummaged inside it until he located the map Dawson had given him. 'There should be a town somewhere nearby,' he muttered, more to himself than to the girl.

In the light of a spluttering match, he scanned it carefully, tracing the trail they had followed this far.

'Sioux Falls,' he said after a few moments. 'Unfortunately, your father hasn't marked any accurate distances on this map but it seems to be the nearest place.'

'I've heard of it.' Belle said faintly. 'A typical frontier town like Cranton but smaller. I'd estimate it to be about three miles from where we are now.'

'Then I reckon that's where we head for. Do you think you can ride?'

'I think so.'

Somehow, with Seth helping her, she managed to get into the saddle. He guessed that the whiskey had helped a little but once the effect of the spirit wore off the pain would come through.

He had hoped they might get a little rest in the shelter of the cave but now it was imperative he should get Belle to a doctor as quickly as possible. Ignoring the slashing rain and vicious lightning strokes that tore across the land, they rode on. To add to their troubles, the horses were skittish and in the pitch darkness it was almost impossible to make out the trail.

They rode with their heads low as the

savage gusts tore at them from all directions. Beside him, Belle struggled to remain in the saddle. Now that the initial shock of the snakebite had worn off some of the pain was coming through. From the corner of his eye, Seth noticed that her lips were pressed tightly together and there were lines of strain over her eyes.

The journey seemed endless and they were both at the end of their strength when Seth lifted his eyes and, through the rain streaming from his hat brim, made out the faint twinkle of lights in the distance below them.

Above the shriek of the wind he yelled, 'We're nearly there, Belle. Just hang on for a little while longer.'

He saw her slight nod as she acknowledged that she had heard him and he saw her lift her head to peer into the enshrouding darkness. Ahead of them the trail led downward but here the ground has been turned into a sticky, viscous mud and they had to move slowly and allow their mounts to find their own way.

It was more than half an hour later when they finally rode into the narrow main street of Sioux Falls. There were few people around and Seth guessed that most of them would be in the various saloons. Halfway along the street, Seth spotted the sheriff's office and reined up the stallion. Getting down, he climbed on to the boardwalk, pushed open the door, and went in. There was a blazing fire burning in a stone grate and the warmth hit him at once.

A tall, grey-haired man sat at the desk, the star on his shirt glinting in the firelight. He glanced up as Seth entered, an expression of surprise on his weather-beaten features.

'You the sheriff?' Seth enquired.

The man nodded, his keen gaze taking in Seth's dripping clothing. 'That's right,' he acknowledged. 'I'm Sheriff Manders. Just who are you, stranger? Seems to me you've ridden quite a ways by the look o' you.'

'We need a doctor.' Seth said evenly. Even as he spoke he knew he would somehow have to explain Belle's presence.

'We?' queried the Sheriff.

'My wife. She's outside. She got bitten by a rattler a little while back, out near the desert. I sucked out the poison from the wound as best I could but I figure the town doctor should have a look at it just to be on the safe side.'

The lawman scraped back his chair and got heavily to his feet. Coming round the side of the desk he went to the door with Seth just behind him. Going forward, Manders stared up at Belle. She was swaying slightly now in the saddle.

'Your husband tells me you've been bitten by a rattler, ma'am.'

Belle gave a quick nod but said nothing beyond flashing an odd look in Seth's direction.

'Then I guess you'd better see Doc Forman.' The sheriff pointed. 'You'll find him on the other side o' the street beside the grocery store unless he's in the saloon.'

'Thanks, Sheriff.' Seth climbed back into the saddle and led Belle's mount through the mud, past three saloons until they found the doctor's surgery. There was a lamp burning inside, throwing a faint yellow glow over the boardwalk.

As he helped Belle down, Seth threw a glance back along the street. The sheriff was still standing outside his office, staring after them. How much of what he had told him did Manders believe, he wondered. Somehow, he pushed his suspicions from his mind only to find them immediately faced by something more.

It seemed highly likely that Bentley's men were holed up in this town if they had figured they must have passed the two of them somewhere in the desert. If that was the case, Manders would almost certainly know of them, and the lawman would have been asked to keep his eye open for a man and a woman riding together.

It was only with an effort that he dismissed that thought from his mind and knocked loudly on the doctor's door. It opened a few moments later and a silver-haired man stood looking out at them.

'Yes?'

'Doctor Forman?' Seth enquired.

'That's right.' The other took in the rain dripping from their clothing and immediately stepped to one side. 'Come inside out of this storm.'

After closing the door behind them, he asked, 'What seems to be the problem, Mister — '

'Claybourne.' Seth said. 'My wife was bitten by a rattler about an hour ago. I've tried to get all of the poison out but — '

'Just sit down in that chair and I'll take a look at it.' Forman indicated the chair by the fire.

Taking off the rough bandage, he examined the wound. Finally, he brought out a thermometer and took Belle's temperature before checking her pulse. Glancing up at Seth, he said, 'Well, I must say you did a good job, Mister Claybourne. I'll clean the wound and put on some antiseptic and then bandage it again. However, I do think it would be wise to rest that leg for a couple of days. Where were the two o' you heading?'

'We have a small homestead about seventy miles north o' here,' Seth told him. He didn't want to have to answer too many questions and two days of rest was more than they could spare if they were to reach Condor Peaks in time to stake Dawson's claim.

'Well one thing's for sure. You won't be ridin' any further tonight. When these storms hit this territory they can last for days. You'd be foolish to try to go on. Get yourself a room in the hotel across the street.'

'I reckon we'll do that.' Seth threw a glance at Belle but her return look was enigmatic and he could read nothing from it.

After thanking the doctor, they crossed the street and went into the small hotel. The desk clerk was a small, wizened man with bushy white hair and eyebrows. He gave them an appraising look as they approached.

'What can I do for you?' he asked in a wheezing voice.

'We need a room,' Seth said.

'And are you intendin' to stay long in Sioux Falls?'

Seth shook his head. 'Not more'n a couple o' days,' he replied. 'Do you have any rooms?'

The clerk gave a toothy smile. 'There ain't many folks who decide to stay in this town.' He eyed them up and down and then pushed the register towards Seth. 'I figure you must be hungry. I'd say you've ridden quite a way.'

'Far enough,' Seth answered sharply. He thrust the register back to the man who glanced closely at it. 'Mr and Mrs Claybourne.'

'That's right. If you could rustle up some grub we'd sure appreciate it.'

Nodding, the other turned and took a key from the wooden rack behind him. 'Number seven,' he said, handing the key over. 'You'll find it at the top o' the stairs at the front.'

Climbing the creaking wooden stairs with Belle close behind him, Seth found the room almost at the end of the long corridor. Unlocking the door, he allowed Belle to enter and then went in, closing and locking the door behind him.

In a moment, Belle turned to face him, her face creased into angry lines. 'How dare you tell these people we're married?' she demanded, a brittle edge to her voice.

Seth spread his hands in an apologetic gesture. 'What else could I tell them? We're travelling together and people are bound to ask questions.'

He allowed his glance to rove around the room. It was fairly large and there was a divan, a bed against one wall and

163

a small sink with a jug of water beside it.

'I'll bed down on the divan yonder,' he said. 'We both need somethin' to eat and then a good night's sleep. Somehow, however, I doubt if I'll get much shut-eye.'

'Why not?'

'You seem to have forgotten that gang who rode past us in the desert. I'm fairly certain they'll be somewhere here in town and they may decide to come looking, especially if they get to talkin' with that sheriff. This is the first place they'll look.'

'So what do you intend to do?'

'First we'll get a bite to eat. Then you come back here and lock the door. I'll get the horses stabled and then take a look around town.'

Going downstairs, they found the desk clerk waiting for them. Leading the way into a larger room, he motioned them to a table. 'I've got plenty of hot stew, meat and potatoes if that will be all right.'

'That will suit us fine,' Belle said, seating herself.

The meal came in a few minutes later and Seth ate ravenously. It seemed an age since he had last eaten a proper meal. When he had finished, he leaned back and rolled himself a smoke. Lighting the cigarette, he said through the smoke, 'Once that leg of yours is fully healed we're goin' to have to travel fast.'

'I can still ride,' the girl answered tartly. 'And,' she added meaningfully, 'I always sleep with a gun under my pillow.'

'You won't need that gun as far as I'm concerned,' Seth replied. 'I've just realized that you're a hard woman, Belle. You haven't got an ounce of softness in you.'

He saw her flinch at that remark and, for a moment, he regretted saying it. She seemed on the point of speaking some further harsh words but then lapsed into silence.

Finishing his smoke, he stubbed out

the cigarette and then followed her back to the room. Once inside, he handed her the key. 'Lock the door after I'm gone and don't open it to anyone but me. You've got a gun. If anyone else tries to get in, use it. You may not get a second chance.'

As he stepped out into the corridor, he heard the key turn in the lock. Going downstairs, he enquired of the desk clerk where they might stable their mounts. The other went to the street door with him and pointed left along the street. 'At the far end,' he wheezed, 'you'll find the livery stables there.'

'Thanks.' Stepping off the boardwalk, Seth grabbed both bridles and led the horses through the clinging mud.

There was a lantern inside the stables and as he went inside, a tall, gangling man came out of the back. From his appearance, Seth guessed that the other was well into his seventies yet he still held himself tautly upright.

'You got room for two more?' Seth asked, noticing that there were several horses stabled there.

'I reckon I can take another two.' The groom jerked his thumb over his shoulder towards two empty stalls at the rear. 'It'll be a dollar a night. That includes food and water.'

'That's fine by me.' As the man led the mounts away after hanging the saddles on a couple of pegs along the wall, Seth said, 'You seem to have quite a lot o' mounts here. More'n I'd have expected for a town this size. You must have several visitors here.'

'Some men rode in durin' the afternoon,' replied the other without turning his head. 'Said they were bounty hunters lookin' for some fella who's wanted for bank robbery some- where east.'

'Did they have any Wanted notices with 'em?'

The groom shook his head as Seth handed over two dollars. 'Never saw any. Usually they ask folks like me who know most o' what goes on in town if I've seen anyone. Tell you the truth, mister, they weren't a talkative bunch at all though they did tell me they were after somebody.'

Going out into the teeming rain, Seth walked slowly back along the street, deliberately keeping into the shadows. He was now certain that Bentley's men were still in town.

At the moment the street seemed totally deserted although there were still a number of mounts tethered to the rails along either side with plenty of noise coming from the saloons. Then the door of the sheriff's office opened and a bunch of men stepped out. Swiftly, Seth pressed himself hard against the nearby wall his right hand close to the Colt at his waist.

The men stood talking together for a while and then separated, moving away into the shadowy alleys on either side of the street. There was no mistaking their purpose. These were the men Bentley and Headers had sent after the girl and himself. Moving quickly, he slipped into a narrow lane between the hardware store and the local bank. At the end, he paused and waited.

The quiet shadow appeared a moment later about three yards to his left. Holding his Colt by the barrel, Seth waited as the man edged silently towards the end of the alley. Before the other had a chance to realize his danger, Seth slammed the butt of the Colt hard against the side of the man's head. He sagged without a sound as Seth caught him and dragged him out of sight through a narrow opening.

A moment later he picked out another faint noise. It was the scrape of heavy boots on hard-packed dirt. Tensely, he waited as the sound came closer, then stopped. There came a hoarse whisper in the darkness. 'Slim! Where the hell are yuh?'

Seth pressed his lips tightly together. Evidently this man had arranged to meet his companion near the end of the lane. There was an uncertain pause on the other's part and then he began to move slowly along the wall. The gunman was, wary now, not taking any chances.

Seth waited tensely until the man drew level with the narrow opening. Ten seconds later he discerned the other's outline. Bringing the Colt down again, he aimed for the man's head but some instinct had warned the other of his danger. He swung sharply away, bringing up his own weapon at the same time.

Seth had no time in which to reverse his hold on the Colt. Swiftly, he brought it down, slamming it hard on his opponent's wrist. The other's gun dropped with a clatter from his nerveless fingers. Before the man could cry out, Seth brought up his other hand and struck a vicious blow across the gunhawk's exposed throat.

A faint bleat of agony came from the man's lips as he fell forward against Seth forcing him backward. Seth's leg caught against the inert body just behind him and he went down, hitting the ground heavily with his left shoulder, the man on top of him. The gunman was hurt but he wasn't finished.

Eyes wide, his lips thinned back across his teeth, the man clamped both hands around Seth's throat, squeezing with all of his strength. Blackness swam before Seth's eyes as he struggled to push the killer away. Somehow, he got his right leg beneath him and heaved upward with all of his remaining strength. For a moment, he thought it would not be enough. Then the other went over on to his side and the weight on Seth's body eased a little.

But the tightly clasped fingers were still around his throat making it impossible for him to draw air into his straining lungs. Then Seth's scrabbling fingers encountered something large and heavy on the ground beside him. With a last despairing effort, he closed his fingers around the barrel of the gun and swung his arm in a vicious arc. The weapon thudded against the man's head with a sickening sound. He went

171

limp, dropping sideways on to the unconscious body of his companion as Seth somehow heaved himself to his knees, sucking air into his chest in long, rasping gasps.

Clawing at the wall he managed to stand upright, swaying as everything spun round him in a dizzying circle. Slowly, everything steadied. There was a thudding in his ears and several seconds fled before he realized what it was — the sound of horses in the main street some distance behind him.

Moving as quickly as he could, he reached the far end of the alley just in time to make out three riders heading swiftly out of town. In spite of the darkness, he recognized one of them at once — the Mexican, Reno, and he had a slim figure lying, apparently unconscious, across the saddle in front of him.

He felt the anger and despair simultaneously. While he had been taking care of those two men, Reno and the other pair had evidently gone into the hotel and somehow managed to abduct Belle. Knowing her, she would have put up a fight but against three of them she wouldn't have had a chance.

For a moment, he stood irresolute. From the direction those riders had taken, he guessed they were heading back to Cranton where they would turn the girl over to Bentley or Henders. With her in their hands, there would be nothing for Dawson to do but agree to their demands.

His only chance was to go after them and hope to get her from their clutches before they reached Cranton but first he had to be absolutely certain they were taking her there. There was also the possibility they might have been given orders to take her to some hideout and he couldn't take the risk of making the wrong decision.

In spite of the pain in his throat, his mind was working clearly and logically now. Turning quickly on his heel, knowing there was little time to be lost, he moved back along the alley to where the two gunmen were.

By the time he reached them, the first man he had slugged was already beginning to come round, moaning low in his throat. Bending, Seth hauled him to his feet, thrusting the barrel of his Colt hard against the man's neck.

'Now you're goin' to talk,' he said, speaking through his clenched teeth, 'and don't try to lie to me. I'd just as soon shoot you here as listen to any lies.'

He saw the man's eyes widen as Seth thrust him hard against the wall. Running his tongue around his lips, the other said hoarsely, 'You won't get anythin' out o' me. By now Reno will have got the girl and there ain't a thing you can do about it.'

'No? I could take you along to the stables, get a rope from my mount, and hang you from one o' the rafters there, hang you slowly so that you take a long time to die.'

'You're no cold-blooded killer,' grunted the other. 'You're bluffin'. Besides, the sheriff is still awake in his office and there are still folk around. You won't kill me in front o' half the town. I've only got to shout and you'll likely find yourself in the jail.'

'You think so?' Seth spun the man around, jamming the gun hard between his shoulder blades. 'Now get movin' and you'll soon find out whether I'm bluffin' or not.'

Watching the other's every move, Seth forced him along the backs of the buildings until they reached the rear of the livery stables. Inside, the groom was still there. He glanced up in surprise as Seth herded his prisoner along in front of him.

To the groom, Seth said calmly, 'Would you bring the rope from my mount.' He saw the oldster hesitate for a moment, then go to the rear of the stalls, returning with the coiled length of rope.

'Are you goin' to just stand there and let this gunslinger hang me?' demanded the killer harshly. 'You'll stand trial as an accomplice to murder if you do.'

The groom gave a toothy grin. 'All depends on what you've done, mister, to make this man want to kill you. Reckon if I was to choose between you as to who deserves to hang, I'd say it was you.'

Before the gunman could say another word, Seth had the noose around his neck and had thrown the other end of the rope over a high beam. Thrusting his face close to the gunman's he said with an ominous quietness, 'Now are you goin' to tell me where Reno and the others have taken the girl?'

As he said it, he gave a sharp pull on the rope. It lifted the other off the ground, the noose tightening around his neck until his eyes bulged. Loosening his hold, Seth lowered him down to the ground. Sucking in a wheezing breath, the man hissed, 'I don't know what the hell you're talkin' about. I — '

Before he could complete his sentence, Seth hauled sharply on the rope once more, letting him swing for half a minute before setting him down. The other stood swaying, struggling to claw at the rope with his fingers.

'Reckon I'll have to hang you then,' Seth said in an ominous tone. 'It's a pity that Reno and the others got away when I guess they were the ones behind all of this.'

He made to pull on the rope for a third time but the killer suddenly gasped, 'All right, all right. Just loosen this rope and I'll tell you what you want to know. Bentley and Henders sent us after you and the girl once he'd discovered you were gone. The orders were to kill you and take the girl alive.'

'And where were you to take her? Back to Cranton?'

He saw the other hesitate and knew that the man was on the point of lying. Seth tightened his grip on the rope. 'I'll hang you, sure as hell, if you don't tell me the truth.'

Swallowing thickly in his bruised throat, the other shook his head. 'No, not back to Cranton. We were to take her up to the old Forbes place in the hills and keep her there until one of us returned to Bentley to tell him we'd got her. Those were the orders we were given.'

Loosening the noose around the other's neck, Seth spun him around and struck him a hard blow on the skull with his Colt. The man fell without a sound. To the groom, Seth said, 'Get my mount ready. Leave him there until he comes round. I don't think he'll make any further trouble.'

A few moments later, the groom returned with his mount. Slipping ten dollars into the man's hand, Seth swung himself up into the saddle. Glancing down, he asked, 'Do you know where this place is?'

'Sure, mister. Instead o' taking the pass through the hills, you turn west after about a mile. There's a trail leading up to the shack. It belonged to old Jim Forbes years ago. He were prospectin' for gold but I reckon he never found any. Ain't nobody seen him for at least three years. Some reckon he left for somewhere back east but that's just talk.'

Guiding the stallion through the stable door, Seth sent it at a run along the narrow street. Now his hope was that Reno would assume that those other two men had taken care of him and there was no fear of them being pursued. That way, Reno might decide to take his time, saving the horses for that long trek across the wilderness.

Clearing the edge of town, Seth stared about him through the teeming rain, searching for the upgrade trail leading through the hills. The storm seemed to be abating slowly as it moved away towards the south but lightning still cracked across the rocks and thunder hammered at his ears.

By the time he came to the narrow pass through the hills, the rain had stopped. Overhead, the sky became clear and starlit. Remembering what the groom had told him, he turned the stallion and swung around the base of the hills urging every last ounce of speed from his mount. He was acutely aware that Reno might have taken the precaution of leaving a man behind to watch this trail. From what he knew, the Mexican took no chances. If there was the smallest possibility that his two companions had failed in the order to kill him, he would know that Seth would come after him. What Reno didn't know was that Seth was now aware of where they had taken Belle.

An hour passed before he sighted the narrow trail to his left that angled sharply up into the hills. In the brilliant starlight it was possible to see it clearly. Reining up his mount, he sat quite still, listening intently for any sound that would indicate where the men were but the silence all around him seemed absolute.

Although it would be possible for the stallion to make that steep upgrade, he decided to go the rest of the way on foot. It was necessarily slow and painful progress and in places it was almost impossible to make out the track where the rain had sent a torrent of water down the steep hillside. Towards the south, the moon came out from behind a bank of cloud, flooding the scene with a pale yellow glow. Moving as quietly as possible he eased his way forward, then came to an abrupt halt. A faint sound reached him out of the shadows that lay ahead. He recognized it at once — the whinny of a horse.

Swiftly, he dropped on to his stomach and wriggled forward, narrowing his eyes against the brilliant moonlight. For a moment, he could make out nothing. Then, lifting his head slowly he saw the wide plateau cut into the side of the hills. In the middle was a large wooden shack. Pale yellow lamplight shone through one of the windows. Evidently, he mused, these men were quite confident they would not be followed here.

He let his pent-up breath go in a long exhalation. That also meant they would not be unduly watchful. There were three horses tethered to a low rail at one side of the shack and, as he watched, an occasional shadow passed across the window. Getting his legs under him, he paused for a moment and then ran across the intervening distance to the hut. Reaching the wall at one side, he pressed himself hard against it, sliding the Colt from its holster in the same movement.

The muffled sound of voices reached him as he stood there but it was impossible for him to make out the words. Cautiously, he edged towards the front of the shack. Just as he reached it, however, the door opened and someone came out and stood for a moment in the swathe of light from inside. Seth recognized the Mexican instantly. There was the spark of a sulphur match as Reno lit a cigar, blowing the smoke into the air.

For a moment, Seth's finger tightened on the trigger of the Colt but then he relaxed. Even if he killed Reno, it was possible either of the other men might kill Belle rather than allow her to go free. Surprise was the only advantage he had. Even though it tautened his nerves to breaking point, he forced himself to stand absolutely still.

After a little while, Reno tossed the cigar butt away, turned, and went back into the shack, closing the door behind him. Cautiously, Seth eased his way along the wall until he reached the window. Very slowly, he leaned forward to peer inside. He made out Belle at once. She was seated in a chair with two of the gunmen beside her. Reno was pacing up and down the room, his hands clasped tightly behind his back.

Now it was just possible to make out what the men inside were saying. Addressing one of the men beside Belle, Reno said harshly, 'You ride back to Cranton, Cal. Tell Henders or Bentley that we have the girl here as planned. Ask them what we're supposed to do next.'

'Can't it wait until mornin'?' Cal replied.

'I said you go now.'

'All right, I'm goin',' retorted the other in a truculent tone. He gave a leering grin. 'It ain't as if she's goin' anywhere.'

As he made for the door, Seth drew back to the edge of the shack. He knew he had to prevent this man from leaving. If he should discover the stallion at the bottom of the trail he would immediately raise the alarm.

The man stepped out of the cabin, still cursing volubly under his breath. Spinning on his heel, Cal made for the horses on the far side of the plateau. Without pausing to think of the possible danger, Seth ran back to the edge of the track, crouching down behind a large, irregular boulder. He knew he daren't risk a gunshot.

Swiftly, he drew his long-bladed knife from its sheath and held it tightly by the tip of the blade. Already, the man had saddled up and was riding towards him, a dark shadow in the moonlight. Seth waited tensely until the other was a mere ten yards away; then he thrust himself sharply to his feet. He glimpsed the rider's hand drop towards the gun at his waist, saw the other's mouth open to yell a warning. Then the knife flashed through the air like a silver streak. It buried itself to the hilt in the gunhawk's chest, the force of the impact pitching him sideways from the saddle.

One foot caught in the stirrups and the next moment the horse was racing down the rocky slope, dragging the man's body with it. Seth waited until the echoes died away and then turned his attention back to the shack. There was no movement from inside. Evidently the two men there had heard nothing apart from the horse leaving.

Breathing a sigh of relief, he returned to his former position. Now there were only two men to take care of but one of them was Reno and he knew the Mexican would undoubtedly kill Belle before allowing her to escape.

Somehow, he had to take them by surprise and that wasn't going to be easy. Despite the fact that both men seemed confident they had not been followed from town, they were still alert. He made to step away from the wall of the shack; then stiffened as something hard was rammed into his back.

A low voice whispered, 'Don't make any funny moves, mister, or this shotgun is liable to go off. Now what the hell are you doin' here on my property?'

Seth turned his head slowly, keepng his hands high. He found himself staring into the lined, whiskered face of an old man, but the eyes that drilled into his were bright and the weapon was rock steady in the other's hands.

'Your property?' Seth murmured. 'Who the hell are you?'

'If you're from Sioux Falls ye know damned well who I am — Jim Forbes.'

6

Precarious Rescue

Seth stared hard at the other, scarcely able to take in what the old man had said. Then he caught Forbes tightly by the arm. 'I need your help,' he whispered. 'Just keep quiet and I'll explain it all.'

For a moment he thought Forbes might use the shotgun but then the oldster allowed him to move away from the shack and into the cluster of stunted bushes that eked out a precarious existence among the rocks. Here they were out of earshot of the men inside the shack.

'There are two gunmen in there,' he explained, 'and they have the daughter of a friend o' mine held captive. The minute I show myself they'll kill her. They're waiting for either Bentley or

187

Henders to arrive from Cranton and then — '

'Herb Bentley?' The other leaned forward and there was something in his eyes that sent a little shiver along Seth's spine.

'That's right. He's tryin' to force her father to sell his spread at a tenth of its worth.'

'Yuh don't need to tell me anythin' about that polecat,' Forbes gritted. 'I know how he works. He took over a small stretch o' land I had west o' here, sent in his men and fired the place.' Forbes threw a quick glance towards the shack. 'Well, I guess if those critters are workin' for Bentley, I'm with you.'

He pointed a finger towards the rear of the shack. 'There's a window at the back. If you get in there you'll find yourself in the kitchen. The door leads into the front room.'

'That's where they've got the girl.'

'Then you wait behind that door until you get my signal.'

'And what will that be?'

The oldster gave a broad grin. 'You'll know when you hear it, young fella. Then come in fast. You got that?'

'I guess so.' Seth was unsure of the other's meaning but there was nothing else he could do but trust him and go along with him. Getting quietly to his feet he ran across to the rear of the shack. The rear window was about three feet from the ground and it opened easily enough as he thrust at it with both hands.

Pulling himself through, he landed lightly on the floor inside. Very slowly, he moved forward, feeling with his hands for any obstacles. His outstretched hand encountered a table and edging forward he could just make out a thin sliver of lamplight through a crack in the door.

Very slowly, he turned the handle, opening it a couple of inches. The two men had their backs to him, Reno standing close beside the girl in the chair. Sucking in a deep breath, he waited, wondering what Forbes intended to do.

He did not have long to wait. A few moments later the door crashed open on squealing hinges and Forbes stood in the doorway, levelling the shotgun at the two men.

'Who the hell are you two, tryin' to take over a man's home?' Forbes demanded.

Slowly, the expression of surprise faded from Reno's face. 'You're that crazy prospector who used to live here.' He threw an oblique glance at his companion. 'Seems we were misinformed, Ben.' To Forbes, he said smoothly, 'If we're trespassin' here, friend, we'll leave. Besides, you ain't goin' to use that gun. If you do, you'll kill us and the girl.'

He took a step forward as if to make for the door, then stopped as Forbes lifted the shotgun a little higher. 'And what's with the girl? Who's she and what's she doin' here?'

'She's run away from her family. We're takin' her back.'

Behind the door, Seth waited tensely,

his Colt drawn. At the moment, Reno was too close to the girl for him to risk making a move. The Mexican could move as fast as a striking snake and could have a knife at her throat within seconds.

'Reckon I'd better ask her.' Forbes moved a little way to one side. For a split second he took his glance off Ben, his attention fixed on Belle. With a sudden lunge, Ben jerked forward in the same moment as Forbes swung the gun. In the small room, the gunshot was deafening.

The gunman had taken the full force of the blast. As he went down, he crashed into the old man sending him falling back against the wall. The next moment, Reno had stepped forward and grabbed Forbes by the throat. 'That was a foolish thing to do, old man,' he hissed. 'Now you're goin' to pay for it. I'm goin' to — '

'You're goin' to do nothing', Reno.' Seth stepped into the room, his gun levelled. 'This is where you reach the end.' He saw the surprise and shock mirrored on the Mexican's swarthy features, saw the gleam of anger in his eyes.

'So those two men failed,' There was no emotion in Reno's voice. 'But you won't shoot me. That isn't the way of men like you. You always want the other man to have an even chance, just to prove you're better than he is.'

'Don't bet on it,' Seth said thinly.

'Don't give him that chance, Seth,' Belle called. 'Shoot him now. If you don't have the guts, give me a gun and I'll do it.'

There was a broad, leering smile on the Mexican's thin lips as he said, 'He won't do that. He's not the kind of man who'd allow a woman to do his killing for him. Are you, *señor*?'

Seth felt a sudden spark of anger deep inside him at the other's mocking words. Without saying anything, he pouched the Colt. 'Go ahead, Reno, make your play. We'll see if you have the guts.'

The other stood quite still, his eyes drilling into Seth's. With his left hand, he made a gesture towards the girl. It was a feint, intended to take Seth's attention off his other hand. Swiftly, his right hand jerked downward towards his own gun. It was halfway out of the holster when Seth's hand struck down towards his Colt.

For a split second, Reno knew what had happened. His eyes bulged as if in sudden shock. Then his knees buckled as he clutched at his shirt where the blood was already beginning to stain it. For a further few moments, he somehow remained on his feet before going down, smashing against the small table as he fell.

Forbes had pushed himself upright. Picking up the shotgun from the floor, he said thinly, 'Well, I guess that's the finish o' them.' Turning to Belle, he asked, 'Are you all right, miss?'

She nodded. To Seth, she said, 'I guess I owe you my life. When those men kicked in the door of the hotel room, I thought they'd already killed you.'

Seth forced a smile. 'I guess we were both lucky that old Jim turned up when he did.'

'What do you two intend doin' now? I got plenty here and you're welcome to stay for the night.'

'Thanks, but unfortunately we've still got a lot o' territory to cover and this delay means we've very little time left.'

Crossing the room, Forbes laid his shotgun against the wall. 'And these two varmints? What do we do with them — ride into town and let the sheriff know what's happened?'

Seth shook his head. 'My guess is that the law there is just as crooked as in Cranton. Better just bury 'em out in the yard someplace and keep quiet about everythin'.'

'But that man who rode back to inform Bentley and the others I was here?' Belle put in. 'Surely he'll talk and when Bentley gets here and finds me gone he may try to get some information from Jim here.'

'Don't you worry your pretty head about old Jim Forbes,' replied the oldster laconically. 'I can take care o' myself. Come daybreak and I'll be up in the hills where he won't find me. But I figure you could do with somethin' to eat and some vittles to take with yuh. I've got a bit stashed away in the shack.'

Half an hour later, with the moon riding high in the clear heavens, Seth and the girl rode back down the narrow, twisting trail, both seated on one of the outlaws' mounts. At the bottom, Seth whistled up the black stallion and climbed into the saddle. There was a dark shadow some hundred yards beyond the rocks and going cautiously forward, Seth came upon the horse with the dead outlaw still hanging by one foot from the stirrups. Bending, he pulled his knife from the other's shirt, wiped the blade on the man's vest and thrust the weapon back into its sheath. Then he dragged him into a clump of mesquite.

Belle watched him in silence. Glancing across at her, he said, 'I had to silence that man Reno sent back to Cranton and that was the only way to do it.'

As he lifted himself into the saddle, he wondered what she was thinking at that moment. So many men had died during the past few days. Now he was wondering if it would ever stop. He was also troubled by thoughts of what might be happening back at Dawson's spread.

* * *

Early the next morning, Clem Henders rode out to Bentley's place, his face set in stern, worried lines. Bentley was already up and standing in the middle of the courtyard when he arrived. Dismounting, Henders said sharply, 'I reckon you can guess why I'm here, Herb. Have you still had no word from Reno?'

Bentley shook his head and tossed his half-smoked cigar away. Inwardly, he

196

was just as worried as Henders but he was determined not to show it. 'You'd better come into the house, Clem. There are matters we have to discuss.'

Handing the reins of his mount to the groom, Henders followed the other inside. He seated himself at the long table and waited while Bentley poured out a couple of drinks before speaking. 'You figure somethin' must've happened to Reno and the others? We should have received word a couple o' days ago. Five men against one man and a girl. It would only take an hour or so to grab the woman and take her to that place in the hills. Unless — ' He paused and looked directly at his companion.

'Unless what?' Bentley demanded.

'I was goin' to say, unless Reno has decided to grab those deeds for himself.'

'Why should he? We both trust Reno and he's a good man at takin' orders.'

Henders sipped his drink in silence for a moment. Then he looked up at his companion, eyeing him closely over the rim of his glass. 'Then it might be that Belle Dawson and this gunslick didn't head for Sioux Falls like we figured. If they decided to keep on ridin' maybe Reno and the others are still followin' them.'

'That's a possibility I've already considered,' Bentley replied gravely. 'But there's a limit to what two riders can carry with 'em and my guess is they wouldn't have sufficient food and water to take 'em much further than Sioux Falls. There isn't another town for more'n forty miles and much o' that territory is nothin' but mountains and desert.'

Henders set down his glass and stared at his hands. 'So you're pretty sure they stayed in Sioux Falls?'

'Pretty sure,' Bentley repeated, pursing his lips.

'So the only other alternative explanation is that this gunman has got the better of Reno and the others.'

Bentley swirled the liquor around in

his glass before nodding. 'Much as I hate to admit it, and find it hard to believe, I'm now comin' around to that way o' thinking.'

'So what ought we to do about it?'

Bentley's smile was a frozen, vicious thing in the pale sunlight just showing through the windows. 'Sometimes, I figure that if somethin's worth doin', you're better doin' it yourself.'

'You mean to go out after 'em yourself?'

'That's exactly what I do mean.' Bentley leaned forward and there was a sudden expression on his face that Henders had never seen before, one he wasn't sure he liked. 'I mean to have that land and if you want your share, then you'll ride along with us.'

'And what do you have in mind for Dawson and his spread?'

'We leave him there for the time bein'. He ain't goin' nowhere with all the men we have watchin' the place. Once we get our hands on those deeds we finish him. I suggest you get ready to ride within the next two hours.'

Henders knew that Bentley would accept no excuse. While there was some merit in what the other said, he, himself, did not relish the idea of riding all that way. Over the years he had grown used to the lavish, easy life in Cranton. The thought of being on horseback for days on end did not appeal to him in the least.

Sighing heavily, he got to his feet, stood staring at his companion for several seconds, then nodded briefly. 'I'll be ready,' he said shortly. 'You want me to bring any o' my men?'

Bentley shook his head. 'I'll pick a couple o' mine. They'll be enough to take this gunslick once we catch up with him.'

★ ★ ★

Taking a narrow hill trail that skirted around Sioux Falls, Seth and Belle struck north-west. The country ahead of them looked sere and desolate in the fading moonlight. They rode in silence, both engrossed in their own thoughts. They were now in territory unknown to either of them. Only the map that Dawson had provided gave them any assurance they were still following the right trail.

Seth could just make out the shadowy smudge of vegetation on the far side of the region but he estimated it was a good ten miles distant. Belle had also seen it and they resigned themselves to a long and dusty ride.

Three hours later, heat was a heavy and uncomfortable weight on their backs and shoulders. The sun blazed in a wide, cloudless sky. Instinctively, Seth tipped his hat forward, shielding his eyes against it. Impatience was strong within him. That delay back at Sioux Falls had drastically shortened the time they had left but he knew better than to push the mounts beyond their limit.

They came upon a narrow stretch of mesquite and sage growing along the banks of a dried-up river bed just before four o' clock in the afternoon. Now the terrain was beginning to lose some of its earlier monotony. Ahead of them stood the lofty peaks of a mountain range that barred their way, stretching several miles along the northern horizon.

Turning to the girl, he said hoarsely, 'We'll rest here for a while. The horses are tired and so are we.'

Gratefully, she lowered herself from the saddle and stood surveying the tall peaks. 'Do we have to climb them?' she asked. 'It will take days to cross those mountains.'

'Maybe, if we're lucky, we'll find a pass through them.' Seth placed his canteen to his lips and allowed a little of their precious water to slide down his parched throat.

Squatting down on the hard-baked soil of the riverbank, Belle sat with her hands clasping her knees. There were lines of strain across her forehead and dark shadows under her eyes.

Seth remained standing, running his gaze along the range. Then he dug inside his jacket pocket and brought out the map. Dawson had clearly marked this mountain range and the river that was now as dry as a bone. Now that he perused the map more closely he noticed that Dawson had shown the trail approaching the range ahead some distance to the left of where he judged they were at the moment.

Stuffing the map back into his pocket, he turned his whole attention on to that particular region and eyed it more attentively. At first, he could make out little to indicate that there might be a place there where they might cross. Then his eye caught a narrow region of dark shadow that could have been a narrow trail snaking its way up the mountainside.

'There!' he said, taking Belle by her arm and pointing. 'That looks like a pass. We'll head in that direction but not until after nightfall. There are a few hours of daylight left and I suggest we try to get some sleep.'

'Wouldn't it be better to ride on now and sleep through the night?'

Seth shook his head. 'It'll be through the night when there'll be the most danger.'

'You think there are still men on our trail. But Reno and the others are dead!'

'Sure. And once no one returns to Cranton, Bentley and Henders are goin' to wonder why. My guess is they'll both come this time with more of their men. They'll never give up so long as they think there's a chance they can stop us. Now let's get some food and sleep. I reckon we're reasonably safe for the moment but when they do come those men will have fresh horses.'

'You seem certain they'll come,' she said gravely, taking some of their food from the saddle-bags.

'I am.' Seth's tone was equally sombre. 'Those men are playin' for high stakes. Neither can afford to lose.'

By the time night came there was a

welcome coolness from the east. Once more the sky was clear and starlit and the moon rose just as they approached the foothills of the range. Ahead of them the tall mountains blotted out much of the sky and there was a wind blowing down from the topmost peaks.

Seth had kept his attention fixed on the dark shadow in the mountainside during the whole of their approach. Now, straining his eyes, he saw that it was, indeed, a steep, narrow track that might give them safe passage for their mounts.

Motioning to the girl, he swung his mount towards their left. Here, the ground was rough and uneven, littered with stones and boulders, and they were forced to pick their way carefully through them.

They had only advanced thirty yards up the steep slope when Belle's mount suddenly shied nervously, almost unseating her. Recalling the rattler that had been the start of all their troubles, Seth pulled the stallion to a rearing halt and peered into the darkness. Nothing seemed to move and there was no ominous rattle to be heard.

Letting his breath sigh through his lips, he motioned the girl to remain absolutely still and climbed down from the saddle, his Colt in his right hand. A moment later, he whirled as a low moan reached him from near a pile of rocks some ten feet away. Warily, keeping the weapon trained on the dark shape, he went forward and then down on one knee.

Striking a match, he stared into a whiskered face, rheumy eyes that looked back at him, dulled with pain.

'What happened, friend?' Seth queried.

The man's lips moved for several moments but no sound emerged. Then he tried to push himself up on his arms, hung there for a moment, before falling back. Belle came forward out of the shadows.

'It looks as though he's been shot,' she murmured in a low whisper, as if afraid of being overheard.

'Sure looks like it. Bring my canteen. If he can talk I want to know what he's doin' here and who did this.'

Placing the canteen to the oldster's lips, he allowed him to drink slowly. A bout of coughing seized him and then, with an effort, he said in a harsh, rattling croak, 'Don't stay on this trail, mister. This is outlaw country. They'll kill you and take everythin' you've got.'

'And what are you doin' in this godforsaken place?'

'Jest a little prospectin'. Folks reckon there's gold here. I was headin' back to Sioux Falls with my mule but they took the lot.' His head lolled back on his shoulders and a long sigh escaped his lips.

'Is he dead?' queried Belle.

'He soon will be.' Seth answered. 'There's at least three slugs in his chest. I'm surprised he's managed to stay alive for so long.' He made to rise but suddenly the old man reached out and grabbed his jacket, clutching at it with a surprising strength.

With a supreme effort, he rasped, 'If you've got to take this trail, mister — be careful.'

'How many of 'em are there?'

For a moment, Seth thought the old fellow had died but then a faint whisper reached him. 'I saw three of 'em but there may be more.' His throat worked as he attempted to say something more but then his head went back and the eyes that stared up at the stars did not see them.

'He's dead,' Seth told Belle soberly, 'but at least he lived long enough to give us a warning.'

'So what do we do now? Do we go on along the pass or try to find another way around these mountains?'

'I'm afraid the latter course would take us several days and if we're to get these deeds to Condor Peaks in time, we only have three days left. We have to go on.'

Very soon, they were within gigantic rock formations that pressed in close against each side of the trail. The serrated peaks soared high above them. The moon lifted clear of the towering summits, throwing a pale wash of yellow light over everything. It also produced dark shadows, in any of which these outlaws might conceal themselves.

Sometime during the early hours of the morning they reached the crest of the pass and were now entering the much smoother downgrade on the northern side. Here the trail was so narrow they were forced to ride in single file, eyes alert for any sign of trouble. Now they were in brilliant moonlight and Seth knew that if there were any outlaws in the vicinity, as the old man had intimated, he and Belle would make perfect targets.

Carefully, he scanned the area all around them. There was a feeling between his shoulder blades that he didn't like. It was something he had experienced before and always it had presaged danger. Yet when it came, it took him by surprise. Without warning, several shots rang out, shattering the stillness.

Grabbing the bridle of Belle's horse, he pulled her mount swiftly behind his, keeping his head low and yelling at the girl to do the same. More shots rang out and the thin screech of ricochets reached them as they pounded down the trail. Turning slightly, he signalled to Belle to ease her way past him as he slowed his mount and pulled it into the side against the rock wall. 'Keep riding!' he called. 'I'll hold 'em off.'

'No. I stay with you.'

'Do as I say.' There was a note of urgency in his voice. As her mount drew level with his, he released his hold on the bridle and slapped the horse hard on the flanks. Rearing, it raced on with Belle holding on tightly.

Dropping swiftly from the saddle, Seth raced for the shelter of a massive rock by the side of the trail. Crouching down, he drew his Colt and waited. Seconds passed and then there came the sound of riders coming rapidly along the narrow track. The first came into sight a few moments later. Bringing up the Colt, Seth squeezed the trigger.

The bullet took the rider in the chest. Throwing up his arms, he twisted sideways in the saddle and then dropped. His body hit the ground and rolled out of sight among the rocks while his mount continued to run on. The men following close behind pulled hard on the reins, bringing their mounts to a skidding halt. There was no space on the narrow track for them to turn. Instead, they did what Seth had expected, sliding from the saddles and running for the rocks, throwing themselves down, out of sight.

'Better give yourself up, mister,' yelled one of them hoarsely. 'We've got you pinned down. You'll be dead before you can reach your mount.'

Pressing his lips close together, Seth remained silent, knowing these men only wanted him to reply to give away his exact position. There were two of them and soon they would try to split his fire.

Turning his head, he allowed his keen gaze to rove over the rocks around him. Both men, he knew, were down behind the rocks on the opposite side of the track. In the shadows it was difficult to make out details but there appeared to be a narrow space at the back of the boulder. In some past geological age it must have fallen from the heights, crashing down the side until it now almost blocked the trail. It might be possible for him to squeeze through and work his way behind the two outlaws.

Very slowly, an inch at a time, he edged around the huge mass of rock. It would not be easy but he had not been mistaken. There was a gap between the boulder and the rock face behind it. Here, it was just possible to stand upright and still remain concealed from the two gunhawks. A few moments later, he reached the end of the gap. Cautiously, he peered around the rock. In the gloom, he could just make out the indistinct shapes of the two men less than ten feet away.

Suddenly, one of them lifted his head and called, 'All right, stranger, you've got ten seconds to come out. Then we're comin'. You can't get away. Better throw out your guns and step out where we can see you.'

No sooner had the man finished speaking, than both men began firing at the place where Seth had been. Slowly, the booming echoes died away. When there was no return fire from him, they got warily to their feet and advanced cautiously along the track, holding their weapons ready.

Seth waited until they had drawn level with his original hiding place and then stepped out on to the track behind them. 'All right, you polecats,' he said harshly. 'Hold it right there.' He saw both men stiffen abruptly as they realized they had been duped. 'Now

drop your weapons and turn around
— slowly.'

Neither man moved. Then Seth's
keen gaze saw the sudden stiffening in
their shoulders and knew they had
reached their decision. Both of them
whirled in the same instant, bringing up
their Colts but Seth had anticipated the
move. The weapon in his right hand
spat blue-white muzzle flame twice.

One of the outlaws went down at
once, falling sideways against his
companion, his gun falling with a
clatter at his feet. He hit the dirt and lay
still. The second remained on his feet,
staring stupidly at the spreading stain
on the front of his shirt. Desperately, he
tried to bring up the Colt in his shaking
hand. He almost made it before a
second bullet took him between the
eyes. The impact threw him backwards,
off his feet, slamming him hard against
the rock. Stepping forward, Seth
prodded both bodies with his boot. He
had felt no remorse at killing these
three men. Undoubtedly, they were

those who had shot down that old prospector he and Belle had met earlier.

The black stallion was standing patiently a few yards down the trail. Climbing into the saddle, Seth paused to reload the Colt and then gigged the mount forward. Belle was waiting for him at the bottom of the trail. An expression of relief flashed across her features as she saw him.

'I heard the shots,' she said, a trifle breathlessly. 'What happened?'

'There were three of 'em just as the old man told us. They're all dead now. I don't think they'll be bushwhackin' any more folk usin' this pass.'

Lifting himself a little in the saddle, he eyed the terrain ahead of them. The moon was now low down in the west and there was a faint red flush over towards the east. It lacked about an hour to dawn, he decided. In the semi-darkness, the trail was just visible where it angled away towards a couple of low hills, covered on both sides by a stand of pine and birch.

Touching spurs to their mounts' flanks, they headed towards them. As Seth had suspected, there was a narrow river running across the trail at this point. It was running fast but did not appear to be too deep. Putting the horses into the water, they waded along the river for a couple of hundred yards before emerging on to the further bank.

Once inside the shelter of the pines, they dismounted. 'We can rest here for a while,' Seth said. 'We've plenty of cover just in case anyone from Cranton is still followin' us.'

'Do you think that's likely?' Belle asked as she seated herself on the soft, springy grass. 'We've seen no sign of them so far.'

'I'm sure of it. But if they're followin' our trail it's possible we may have thrown them off by takin' the horses downstream.'

'But even that might not be to our advantage,' the girl said helplessly. 'It will just mean they reach Condor Peaks before we do and they'll be lying in wait for us. We have to push on as quickly as we can. There are still almost fifty miles to go and only three days in which to get there.'

'I know.' Seth took out Dawson's rough map again and studied it closely in the growing morning light. Replacing it in his pocket, he rolled a smoke, lit it, and then said, 'Seems that much o' the country from now on is like this. There's a town your father has marked, some place called High Springs. It's about thirty miles or so further on and the only one close to Condor Peaks. I suggest we make for that once we've rested and had somethin' to eat.'

★ ★ ★

It was early afternoon when Herb Bentley and Clem Henders rode into the small clearing at the top of the rocky trail and came in sight of the crude wooden shack. It had been a long hard ride from Cranton and Henders was still cursing volubly as he tried to find a comfortable position in the saddle.

Bentley sat quite still for a full minute, surveying the apparently deserted building, his glance taking in everything. Finally he lifted his right hand to signal to the two men who accompanied them. 'Hal and Slim, go take a look around that place. I want to know if anyone has been here in the past few days.'

Slim looked dubious. 'If there is anyone at home, boss, they'll have us in their sights from that window.'

'We'll cover you,' Bentley snapped. 'Now get goin'.'

The two men slid from their saddles and drew their guns as they ran forward, their heads down, weaving from side to side to present a more difficult target to anyone who might be inside. Bentley saw them reach the wall, one man on each side of the doorway.

Hesitating for a moment, Slim then edged sideways and aimed a kick at the door. It burst open at the impact and he ran inside with Hal close on his heels.

Taking out a cigar, Bentley bit off the end and placed it with an exaggerated movement between his lips. Lighting a match, he waved it slowly over the tip. He was not expecting any trouble but the fact that Reno and the others did not appear to be here worried him.

Five minutes later, both men came out, pouching their guns and shaking their heads.

'There's no one here, boss,' called Hal loudly, 'but it looks as if someone's been — and not more'n a day or two ago.'

'It must have been Reno and the others,' Henders said harshly. 'I know this place. The old guy who owned it pulled out and left years ago. So who else could it have been?'

'That doesn't worry me,' Bentley replied coldly. 'What does worry me is where they are now and is that gunman who was with Belle Dawson still alive.'

Dismounting, he walked towards the shack with Henders close behind. Inside, his keen gaze took in the small table and two chairs with an iron bed pushed hard against the far wall. Small items of prospecting equipment were stacked in a pile in one corner. But it was the items on the table that took his immediate attention.

There were the remains of a meal and a close examination told him that the food was quite fresh, certainly not more than a few days' old.

To Henders, he said coldly, 'Then if Reno is still alive, he's somewhere out there with the girl and if not — '

He was interrupted by a sudden shout from outside. Going to the door, he glanced out. Hal had walked around to the side of the shack. Now he was standing ten yards away, pointing urgently towards a spot where a single stunted pine grew close to the rocks. Going out, Bentley walked over to him.

'It looks to me as though someone has been buried here and not long ago,' Hal muttered. 'That soil is freshly dug.'

Bentley scratched his chin where the two-day growth of beard was beginning to itch uncomfortably.

'And there are two of 'em.'

'That gunman and the girl?' Hal suggested.

'Perhaps. Or Reno and one other of my men.'

'I thought your orders were that the girl wasn't to be harmed,' Henders butted in.

'So they were.' Bentley spoke thin, through his teeth. 'But who knows what happened here?' He experienced a sudden surge of anger. He felt utterly confused and it was not a sensation he was used to. What he had considered to be a simple course of action, send out five of his best men to hunt down one man and a girl, had now turned into a veritable nightmare for him. Events seemed to be happening that were completely out of his control.

Swinging sharply on Henders, he gritted, 'It would seem there's nobody I can trust to carry out the simplest orders. Now there's only one thing we can do.'

'We ride back to Cranton and deal with Dawson?'

'No. We push on to Condor Peaks. I realize the horses are tired but if Belle Dawson is still alive and riding with that hired killer, then their mounts are just as tired. Everyone back in the saddle. We're ridin' out.'

Grumbling under his breath, Henders heaved himself on to the back of his mount. Every muscle and bone in his body ached as if he had been kicked by a maddened bull. But he knew that when in his present mood, Bentley was capable of doing anything and he had no choice but to go along with him.

Strung out in a loose bunch, they made their way slowly down the treacherous track. In the lead, Bentley made to urge his mount forward and then stopped as Henders cried out, 'There's a body yonder, nearly hidden among those bushes!'

Bentley was the first to reach it. Bending, he turned the man over, then stared up at the others. 'It's Cal.'

'Had he been shot?' Henders asked, not wanting to step down and see for himself.

'Hell — no. He's been stabbed through the chest.' Bentley stared around him, feeling the sense of confusion rising again in his mind. 'And I see no sign of the knife.'

He checked the other's Colts. 'His guns are still in their holsters and they haven't been fired.' Straightening up, he looked around at the others. 'There's somethin' here that doesn't add up. Whoever did this must've taken him by surprise.'

Henders cast an apprehensive glance towards the rocks nearby as if expecting to see the killer standing there. Bentley noticed the other's action. 'Whoever the killer is, he ain't within ten miles of us, Clem. Cal's been dead for several hours. My guess is that he was on his way to tell me they had the girl here and someone killed him to prevent me from knowing.'

'Then you figure those two graves up

yonder are Reno's and one o' the others?' queried Hal.

Bentley returned to his mount and swung himself into the saddle. 'It's sure beginnin' to look that way. Seems we've underestimated this gunman who's ridin' with Belle Dawson. The sooner we catch up with him, the better.'

7

The Night Stalker

A day and a half of hard travelling brought Seth and Belle within sight of High Springs. From their vantage point on a tall bluff covered with second growth timber, they looked down on a town sprawling within the bend of a wide river. It was, Seth reckoned, somewhat smaller than Cranton or Sioux Falls and in the late morning sunlight, there was very little sign of any activity.

'There doesn't seem to be much goin' on,' Seth observed. 'I suggest we put up for the night in a hotel — if there is one. We'll make it to Condor Peaks in about five hours from here. If we set out early tomorrow mornin' there ought to be plenty o' time to register your pa's claim.'

Belle looked at him with a strange light in her eyes. 'You still mean to do that for him?'

Seth gave a wry smile. 'You've had me figured for someone who intends to take this land for himself. That's what you've been thinking to yourself ever since we set out.'

The girl flushed. 'I'll admit I've got you wrong, Seth. To be truthful I had you down as just another sodbuster, taking everything you could. But out here, along the frontier, it's not easy to trust anyone. I'm sorry for how I acted at the beginning. After all that's happened on the way here, I believe you're a truly honest, decent man.'

Seth nodded. 'But we haven't finished yet. Bentley won't let this land slip through his fingers if he can possibly help it. My guess is he's on our trail — and not too far behind.'

They set their mounts to the downgrade and half an hour later entered the narrow street running through the middle of High Springs.

Casting an eye along the dusty road, Seth noticed that most of the buildings seemed old and dilapidated. Wooden slats were missing from the boardwalks and the signs outside the two saloons all needed a fresh coat of paint. Clearly, this was a town that was dying on its feet.

The few folk on the boardwalks eyed them curiously as they rode slowly by. Halfway along they made out the only two-storey building in the entire town. As Seth had guessed, it was the hotel. He reined up the stallion in front of it and helped Belle down.

'It ain't much to look at,' he muttered, 'but I guess it'll do for one night.'

Going inside, they found a small, stooped man seated in a chair behind the desk. He glanced up as they approached and then pulled himself to his feet, an expression of undisguised surprise on his thin, angular features.

'You got two rooms available for one night, friend?' Seth enquired.

'Sure, sure.' The other nodded his head in a series of stiff jerks.

Seth glanced down at the desk. 'You got a register here?'

'Register?' The look of surprise on the man's face deepened. 'We don't have such new-fangled ideas here in High Springs. You git the rooms and pay for 'em now.'

'Can you provide us with a meal?' Belle asked.

The man shook his head. 'There's only me workin' here now and I ain't got any time for preparin' food. You'll get somethin' to eat over at the restaurant across the street yonder.'

'But there is some place where we can stable our mounts for the night?' Seth tried to keep the sarcasm from his voice.

'Yeah. A couple o' blocks along the street. Old Mal will stable 'em for you.'

After seeing to the horses, they walked into the small restaurant. The room was dim with very little sunlight managing to penetrate the thick layer of dust on the windows. The place was empty apart from two oldsters seated at a table near the far wall. Seth chose one so that he sat with his back to the wall, facing the door. It was an old habit but one that had saved his life on a number of earlier occasions.

When it came, however, the food was good with heaped plates of bacon, potatoes, eggs and sausages. They ate without talking, both ravenous from the long journey. Once they had finished, Seth stepped outside. Here, the heat was stifling. The air lay unmoving over everything like the inside of an oven.

Leaning his shoulders against a wooden post, he rolled a cigarette watching everything that was happening through lowered lids. He was still unable to shake off the feeling of imminent danger. The town seemed peaceful enough, almost deserted. A couple of riders came in from the north, their clothing dust stained. Seth watched closely as they tethered their mounts outside one of the two saloons and stepped inside.

Belle came out a moment later to join him. 'Do you see any sign of trouble?' she asked anxiously. Evidently the same feeling had affected her. They were now so close to their goal that the idea that something might happen to prevent them reaching it seemed to be continually in her mind.

'Nope.' Lighting the cigarette, he inhaled deeply. 'Everythin' seems normal.'

'But you think something is going to happen now that we've got this far?'

He gave a slight nod. 'I guess it comes from bein' in the war. You're always waitin' for an attack to come and you keep wonderin' where and when it'll strike.'

The town remained quiet throughout the long hot afternoon and by the time night came Seth was feeling a little easier in his mind. Going up to their rooms Seth warned Belle to keep her door locked.

In his own room, he pulled a chair over to the window and sat in the darkness, keeping watch on the street below. The only sound came from the saloons in the distance. Some time later, he must have fallen asleep for he woke with a start, suddenly tensed and alert. Something outside had intruded upon his senses bringing him tautly upright in the chair.

Lifting his head a little, he peered down into the dark shadows that lined the empty street. As far as he could determine, it was deserted. Then, a few moments later, there was a movement at the far end where the desert trail entered the town, Narrowing his eyes, he made out the indistinct shapes of four riders strung out in a line across the narrow street.

As they came closer, he recognized the two men in the middle. Herb Bentley and Clem Henders! The other two men he guessed were gunslingers hired by one of the two men. The riders were moving slowly, watching both sides of the street.

Getting swiftly and silently to his

feet, Seth crossed to the door and opened it quietly, slipping out into the corridor. He knocked quietly on Belle's door, praying that she would have the sense not to light the lamp. A moment later, he heard her soft voice on the other side of the door.

'Who is it?'

'It's me, Seth. Open up.'

A key turned in the lock and a moment later, the door opened. 'What is it, Seth?' she asked in a low whisper.

'Bentley and Henders have just ridden into town with a couple of their men. They certainly didn't waste any time trackin' us down.'

'Where are they now?'

'My guess is they've ridden for the livery stables to put up their mounts for the night. Then I figure they'll come here.'

'So there's no chance of reaching our horses and making a run for it?'

'I'm afraid not.' Remembering what had happened the last time in Sioux Falls, Seth went on, 'Better get yourself ready and we'll slip out the back way. At the moment, they're not sure that we're here.'

Less than five minutes later, they were in the open at the rear of the hotel. There was no sound from the direction of the main street but Seth knew that Bentley and the others were there, no doubt debating their next move.

Making no sound, he edged along the narrow alley at the side of the hotel, Belle close on his heels. Swiftly, he threw a quick glance along the street. The whole town was in darkness except for the yellow glow that emanated from the lively stables. Outlined against the light of that lamp, he made out the silhouettes of several figures.

A few moments later, three of the men emerged. Bentley and Henders were easily recognized. Seth smiled grimly to himself. Evidently, Bentley was taking no chance. He had left one of his men in the stables to watch the horses. There was also no doubt that he had recognized the big back stallion and now knew that he and Belle were somewhere in the town.

Turning to the girl, Seth said harshly, 'We've only one chance, I'm afraid. We have to take them here.'

The girl's face was a pale blur in the dimness. Her features were expressionless but he knew she had grasped his meaning. 'I'm ready,' she replied steadily. 'I know what we have to do.'

'Good.' He gave a jerky nod. Easing the Colts in their holsters, he waited until the three men were less than fifty yards away and then stepped out into the middle of the street. Henders saw him at once and gave a loud yell of warning.

Seth called directly to the tall man in the middle of the trio. 'This is as far as you go, Bentley.'

He saw the other stop and jerk his head up. For a moment, there was silence. Then Bentley shouted hoarsely, 'I've got no quarrel with you, mister, whoever you are. All I want now are those deeds. There's been enough killin'. Just hand 'em over and then ride on, both of you.'

'Not a chance,' Seth called back. He knew the other was stalling for time.

The gunman on Bentley's left began to move slowly towards the boardwalk. In a shaking voice, Henders suddenly yelled, 'I want no part in this. Bentley forced me into comin' and — '

'Shut your snivellin' mouth,' Bentley yelled. As if this had been a prearranged signal both he and the gunman beside him went for their guns. The gunhawk was lightning fast. In an instant, however, Seth had loosed off a shot that took Bentley in the chest and at the same moment, he dropped to his knees, swinging his Colt towards the hired gunman.

At once he heard the vicious hum of the bullet as it passed within an inch of his head. Then a second shot rang out. Before the gunman could squeeze the trigger again, he swayed sideways. The starch went out of his legs as he fell against the wooden railings, his weapon falling at his feet.

Seth turned slowly. Belle had stepped out behind him and she was holding a smoking Colt in her right hand. Giving her a quick nod of thanks, he turned his attention back to the street. There was no sign of Henders. During the brief gunfight he had disappeared into the shadows of a side alley.

A couple of seconds later, more shots rang out from the far end of the street. Grabbing Belle around the waist, Seth thrust her on to the boardwalk, hard against the wall, cursing himself for having forgotten about the man stationed in the livery stables. One glance was enough to tell Seth that the other was well concealed. Immediately, he weighed up the situation.

From where he was, the killer commanded an excellent view along the entire street and could pick off anyone trying to rush him. A further danger was that by now several of the citizens of the town had been aroused and lights showed in most of the windows.

'Stay here,' he said softly.

'What are you going to do?' For a moment, he thought he detected a little tremor in her voice.

'I've got to get that *hombre* in the stables before we have the whole town on our necks. Wait for my signal and then fire a shot at the stable entrance. When I signal again, run for the horses. We have to leave here as quickly as we can.'

'Watch yourself, Seth.'

'I will.' Bending low, he waited for a moment and then ran across to the far side of the street. Reaching the boardwalk, he flung himself down as a couple of slugs struck the wooden planks just behind him. A third bullet hit the wall of the building and ricocheted into the distance.

Then he was worming his way forward, pulling himself along with his elbows. Now he could see through the open door of the stables. The man was just visible to one side. Very slowly, he lifted himself and waved an arm. The shot from Belle's gun struck the side of the door and in that instant the man jerked himself forward and aimed swiftly along the street to where he reckoned Belle was concealed.

Taking careful aim, Seth squeezed the trigger. The man twisted but remained standing, clinging to the doorpost with one hand as he tried to turn to face Seth. For several seconds, he stood there. Then his hand fell away as he tried to stagger into the street. But the bullet had found its mark. His head went forward and then he went down, sprawled in the entrance with his legs twisted under him.

Even before Seth raised his hand to signal to Belle she was running along the boardwalk towards him.

Stepping over the dead man, they found their mounts and quickly threw on the saddles. As he swung up on to the stallion, Seth noticed the groom backed into a corner, an expression of utter terror on his lined features. Seth tossed a coin in his direction.

'Take this for your trouble, old man,' he called. 'See to it that this *hombre* is buried on Boot Hill. There are a couple of others in the street.'

As they cleared the stable entrance, Seth noticed signs of activity in the street. Several people had come running out and were staring in all directions, some carrying rifles. Seth didn't wait to see what was about to happen. Motioning to Belle, they touched spurs to their mounts' flanks and a moment later were racing along the narrow, half-seen track towards the north.

Several shots followed them but in the darkness the townsfolk were shooting at shadows.

'Do you think any of them will follow us?' Belle called.

'I doubt it. A lot will depend upon what Henders tells them once he discovers, we're gone and the others are dead. It's a pity we didn't get him with the rest of 'em but it can't be helped now.'

Daybreak found them on the edge of a wide stretch of rich, lush grassland interspersed by several small, swift-running streams. Eyeing the terrain around them, Seth said soberly, 'If this is somethin' like that land your Pa bought, I'd say a man could spend the rest of his days here, raising some o' the best beef in the country.'

Belle nodded. 'He sometimes spoke of coming out here but much of the time he couldn't make up his mind whether to live here or sell it at a good price to the railroad.'

'Guess we won't know what he intends doin' until he gets here and that could be some time yet.'

'He'll be here,' said Belle fiercely, 'just as soon as the doctor says he can travel.'

'You don't have to convince me o' that. He's one o' the most stubborn and determined cusses I've ever met.' Shading his eyes, Seth stared into the distance to where a small cluster of buildings showed on the skyline.

A little over an hour later they reached their destination. Condor Peaks was clearly a place that had only recently sprung into existence. It was little more than a cluster of scattered buildings on either side of a dirt road. Seth ran his gaze over it and smiled grimly to himself. Whoever had given it its name clearly had a sense of humour for the nearest mountains were just visible on the horizon more than thirty miles distant.

Turning to Belle, he said, 'First thing we do is find a place where we can stay. Then we locate the Land Registry office and stake your Pa's claim. I reckon that once we've done that, all we can do is wait until he gets here.'

He saw that she was looking directly at him and there was an expression on her face he had never seen before. 'You really are going to put my father's name on that document.' It was more of a statement than a question.

'I gave him my word,' Seth replied. 'I don't intend to go back on it.'

She seemed to be having difficulty in finding the right words but finally she said, 'Then I guess I owe you an apology. It would seem there are some honest men around, after all.'

'Thanks. Now let's see if this place has a hotel of any kind.'

The hotel, when they eventually found it, was situated a little way back from the main street, a two-storey building that looked to have been more recently built than most of the others. To Seth's surprise, the man behind the desk was young and there was a pretty blonde woman standing behind him.

'Do you have a couple of rooms?' Seth asked.

'How long do you intend staying in Condor Peaks?' the man asked. 'His tone implied that very few people ever stayed long in the town.'

'A week, possibly two,' Belle interrupted. 'At least until my father gets here from Cranton.'

The other pushed the register towards them. Almost apologetically, he said, 'As you can guess we don't get many folk as far north as this. My wife and I came here a year ago, hoping this town might grow, especially if the rumours are true and the railroad may be coming through.'

'You never know,' Seth agreed laconically, 'but with all o' this good farmland around here, it might grow even without the railroad.'

The woman led them up the wide stairs to their rooms. As she made to leave, Belle asked, 'Could you tell us where the government registry office is?'

'The registry office. You'll find it at the far end of the street. It stands on its own.'

Half an hour later, Seth and Belle made their way to the far end of the street. The office was easily recognizable. There was an oil lamp burning inside. Taking the deeds from his jacket pocket, Seth made for the door. He had almost reached it when a voice he instantly recognized said softly, 'Just hold it right there, mister. If you don't mind, I'll take those deeds.'

Seth halted abruptly in his track. Clem Henders! He cursed himself inwardly for not having remembered that the man was still alive.

'Now turn around very slowly and keep your hands where I can see 'em. You have ten seconds to hand over those deeds or the girl gets it first. I'm sure you wouldn't like that to happen.'

Gritting his teeth, Seth stared at the other. Henders had a Colt in his right hand and Seth knew he would certainly carry out his threat. 'You won't get away with this,' he said through tightly-clenched teeth. 'They'll never believe you're Jeb Dawson.'

Henders smiled broadly. 'There's more chance of them believin' me than a drifter like you. You have five seconds.' The gun swung slightly to cover Belle and Seth saw the man's finger tighten on the trigger. He knew it would be impossible for him to draw his own gun and beat a speeding bullet.

Then something happened to Henders's flabby features. His eyes became

244

even more staring and he began to sway on his feet. There was a sudden gush of blood from his mouth and the Colt slipped from his fingers.

'What — ' Wonderingly, Seth tried to make sense, of what had occurred. Then he noticed the knife protruding from between Henders's shoulders and, a second later, a tall figure stepped into view twenty yards away.

'Grey Shadow!' Belle's exclamation was a whisper of astonishment. 'How did you get here?'

The Indian came forward, bent, and pulled out the knife, wiping it on the dead man's coat before thrusting it back into his belt. 'When your father hear that both Bentley and Henders had left town, he sent me to follow them. It was not difficult. My pony can travel far faster than those of the white man and for much longer.'

'Then I guess we owe you our lives,' Belle replied. 'And how is my father?'

'The doctor said he would be well enough to travel in two days. By now, he'll be on his way.'

Seth stared down at the body, then turned on his heel and walked over to the office. Belle made to follow him, then stopped. There were conflicting emotions in her mind. Five minutes later, Seth came out and handed her the official document. At the bottom he had scrawled her father's name.

Looking up, she said softly, 'Somehow, I don't think my father will have you arrested for forging his name.'

* * *

Five days later, Seth spotted the small band of men riding towards them. Behind Dawson were six others.

As Jeb dismounted, Belle ran forward and threw her arms around him. 'You finally made it,' she said breathlessly. From her pocket, she took the legal document and gave it to him. 'Seth signed your name at the bottom,' she said.

'I never doubted he would,' her father

replied, throwing a quick glance in Seth's direction. 'I've always prided myself on bein' a good judge o' character.'

As they walked towards the hotel, he went on, 'I've made my mind up about what I'm goin' to do. I've already sold the spread to one o' the other ranchers in Cranton and I ain't sellin' to the railroad. This is mighty good country and this is where I mean to stay. These boys here have all agreed to stay and help me build a ranch out here and work for me.'

His sharp-eyed glance fell on Seth. 'And when I'm gone, I figure I'll be leavin' the place in good hands.'

'But you can't think o' leavin' it to me,' Seth protested.

Dawson moved towards the hotel door. Pausing, he looked back. 'To *both* of you.'

Belle moved a couple of steps closer to Seth. As her hand slid into his, she murmured, 'You know, I think that sometimes my father can see things a lot clearer than you.'

We do hope that you have enjoyed reading this large print book.

Did you know that all of our titles are available for purchase?

We publish a wide range of high quality large print books including:
Romances, Mysteries, Classics
General Fiction
Non Fiction and Westerns

Special interest titles available in large print are:
The Little Oxford Dictionary
Music Book, Song Book
Hymn Book, Service Book

Also available from us courtesy of Oxford University Press:
Young Readers' Dictionary
(large print edition)
Young Readers' Thesaurus
(large print edition)

For further information or a free brochure, please contact us at:
Ulverscroft Large Print Books Ltd.,
The Green, Bradgate Road, Anstey,
Leicester, LE7 7FU, England.
Tel: (00 44) **0116 236 4325**
Fax: (00 44) **0116 234 0205**

THE FENCE BUSTERS

Tom Gordon

The open Texas range was the finest cattle-land in the world. But when some forward thinking men erected fences, others suffered the consequences as their cattle were deprived of water and the best grassland. These men turned night-riders, destroying the long fence lines. Lives were lost and property ruined . . . Young and reckless, Tom Midnight joined the ranks of the fencers; his flaming guns were there to argue with the eastern speculators, seeking to fan the flames of conflict.